Beneath The Weeping Willow

M. L. NIETZEL

Beneath The Weeping Willow
Copyright © 2024 by M. L. Nietzel.

All rights reserved. No part of this publication may be reproduced, distributed, or transmitted in any form or by any means, including photocopying, recording, or other electronic or mechanical methods, without the written consent of the publisher. The only exceptions are for brief quotations included in critical reviews and other noncommercial uses permitted by copyright law.

MILTON & HUGO L.L.C.
4407 Park Ave., Suite 5
Union City, NJ 07087, USA

Website: *www. miltonandhugo.com*
Hotline: *1- 888-778-0033*
Email: *info@miltonandhugo.com*

Ordering Information:
Quantity sales. Special discounts are granted to corporations, associations, and other organizations. For more information on these discounts, please reach out to the publisher using the contact information provided above.

Library of Congress Control Number:		2024918923
ISBN-13:	979-8-89285-293-7	[Paperback Edition]
	979-8-89285-294-4	[Hardback Edition]
	979-8-89285-295-1	[Digital Edition]

Rev. date: 10/18/2024

CHAPTER

1

The wind sings as it gently wraps itself around the rough bark of the largest tree in the southern hemisphere, the Great Willow Tree. With a trunk over twenty feet in diameter, this natural beauty pierces the heavens nearly four hundred feet above its twisting roots. A sacred sentinel of tranquility, its majestic presence commands attention. Its long, pendulous branches sweep gracefully downward, like cascading waterfalls frozen in time, forming an intricate curtain of verdant foliage that sways gently in the breeze. The leaves flutter delicately, like whispers in the wind, each a testament to the tree's vitality. Beneath its sprawling canopy, a sanctuary of serenity is formed, inviting those around it to seek refuge from the heat of the sun. The trunk, gnarled with age, weaves a tapestry of stories etched by the passage of time. Amidst its draping branches, the tree appears to weep, with slender tendrils of leaves falling gracefully toward the earth, evoking an aura of melancholic beauty. The giant weeping willow, a living artwork of nature, exudes a sense of quiet elegance and a timeless connection to the environment it graces

For centuries, the wood elves have protected this sacred tree from the violence of the outside world. Legend tells us the tree holds the key to the elvish ancestral history from time long before living memory. It's their connection to the world beyond the eternal slumber at the end of one's lifespan. To the elves, it is their lifeforce; their solitary guardian. To others, it's a dangerous obstacle to domination. Because of this, many have tried to destroy the tree to acquire power over the world. The loss of life is inevitable during such times, but there is honor in protecting what you believe in until the very end. This belief is engraved deeply within the souls of all wood elves; the young and the old, the wise and the naive, the meek and the bold— everyone.

Indeed, there is honor in protecting your beliefs — but belief is not unaffected by a person's heart. Kind or cruel, merciful or vengeful. Good or evil. Shadows obfuscate, bringing forth questions, speculation, seeding doubts. Is there honor in a needless death, for an avoidable conflict? What of corruption, could it be sprouting, secretly, just out of sight? Just as immutable as the rise and fall of the sun, so too is change. In the unpredictable tapestry of life, the threads of transformation are woven with both delicate fragility and remarkable resilience. Time shapes all, molding our perspectives and priorities, and altering the very essence of who we are. Once steadfast convictions may evolve, with new experiences and insights reshaping our understanding of the world. Amidst this ever-shifting landscape, there remains, yet still, an enduring core of life connecting us all— a thread of empathy that transcends transient changes, binding us together in our shared journey. Those who have severed that extraordinary connection no longer deem themselves alive, but rather trapped in a vortex of darkness and despair, hungry and desperate for escape. The absence of the profound interplay between shared experiences and mutual understanding creates a void that cannot be easily filled. Like ships lost at sea, they drift through life's currents without the anchor of meaningful connections. The world around them may continue to spin, but it becomes a colorless backdrop, devoid of the vibrancy that genuine relationships bring. The organism's experience is inherently woven with threads of companionship, empathy, and belonging. To sever those ties is to lose touch with the very essence of what it means to be alive— to be a part of the intricate web of emotions, experiences, and shared moments that define our existence. All that's left of those who have isolated themselves from the webs of life in search of power, is a hollow empty shell buried deep below the earth's surface.

Despite the uncertainties and challenges that populate our existence, there is one constant that remains unwavering. Regardless of the tragedy, the sun continues to rise each morning, continuing the cycle of life and death.

"Ilana, dear, it's time for supper, hurry down before it gets cold," a lovely voice cooed, soft as silk and pure as a turtle dove.

Being my mother, I find it easy to forget that she is the queen of our colony. It is strange to remember it in moments like this, but the kind warmth in her voice even as she projected it for me to hear is queenly, even in subtlety.

"I'm on my way down Mother, give me another minute," I called back to her as my ink-smeared pen finished its final stroke along my rough journal paper. As I stood up to venture downstairs for family supper, I stretched my aching body and, as I swept my hair back, I noticed, with some annoyance, that ink had stained my hair.

As I quickly rubbed at the noticeable black mar on my silken blonde hair, I wondered after the meal I was delaying. I flicked the poorly cleaned strand back behind my shoulder and hoped we would not be having roast lamb. Again. I felt a brisk light breeze twirl beneath my dress alerting me of an open window. I smiled at the crisp spring sun peaking over the sea of trees one last time before conceding to the night's awakening.

"Come, Ilana, sit with us. We're celebrating with a feast dedicated to your brother's return from the eastern valley yesterday. Your food will become cold if you don't hurry," my father called out, with a hint of annoyance at my lack of haste.

"Now, now, Aldon. Must we rush her and risk her pretty skin? We wouldn't want her to fall." My mother called out to him as she gently took his hand in hers, "Admiring the evening is a gift that we are capable of in this time of peace. We should all take a moment to enjoy it."

"Sorry," I mumbled, head down to hide that my cheeks were flush with embarrassment. I scurried to the dining table and sat down beside my two brothers, who both chuckled at my flustered behavior.

After I collected myself, my eyes widened and sparkled as I admired the beautiful feast that was spread along the long table. Before me was a shining, golden roasted duck resting on a bed of greenery, presented on fancy china. To the left was a mountain of fluffy mashed potatoes topped off by various creamy streams of gravy and glistening green scallions. To the right rested two glass bowls. The larger bowl contained a forest of lettuce leaves, shimmering cherry tomatoes, and several other vegetables combined to make a deluxe chopped salad, topped off by a beautiful oily dressing. The smaller bowl contained steamy, bite-sized croquettes, golden brown as the desert sands of Quenntebis.

"The food looks amazing tonight," I exclaimed in awe, "the chief has really outdone herself this time."

"Wow, Little Lala is actually excited for supper? I don't think I've ever heard her compliment the chef with such enthusiasm," my older brother Calem grinned as he rubbed my right shoulder.

"I would compliment them more if we had some variety," I retorted as I felt my face grow hot.

"Indeed." My eldest brother, Reed, agreed. His gentle smile was slightly visible past Calem's head. "I haven't seen her this excited in a while. It's heartwarming in a way."

"Of course you would think that," my sister, Freya, retorted with a dramatic eye roll.

"Sometimes I really don't think she's truly grown up yet," my eldest sister, Tauriel, teased.

I blushed as I sunk back into my chair. My sisters began giggling, which caused a chain reaction of laughter all around the table as we began eating our evening meal.

"So Calem, was your venture into the eastern valley successful?" I asked curiously, breaking the silence.

He swallowed, then answered, "Indeed it was."

"What was it like there, dear brother? I've never been, but I've always been curious," Tauriel asked, gently as if her voice was cradling an infant child.

"There are these ginormous mushrooms that stand as tall as trees," he started, his voice raising with his hands as he gestured to indicate their size, "and the livestock! They were bigger than you and I combined!"

"That's absolutely marvelous," Freya said as her eyes sparkled with astonishment and wonder.

"The flowers were big enough to make a small home inside," he said, standing from his chair as his theatrics continued beyond the bounds of the table.

"No way," I said, rolling my eyes, unconvinced that the story he spewed from his tongue was true.

"Lala, I'm being honest," he assured me.

"Okay, okay."

"Anyway, the magical border was intact, father. We do not need to worry," said Calem, sitting back down and shifting his attention to duty.

"Very good, my son. These checkups twice a year are very important to ensure that balance is maintained."

From the depths of his seasoned chest, my father's jolly voice resonated like the soothing rumble of distant thunder, carrying with it the wisdom of ages and the warmth of paternal affection. Each syllable was a harmonious blend of authority and geniality, a melody that could command the attention of a court yet cradle the hearts of his loved ones. It was a voice that held the echoes of countless stories and a legacy of leadership, a resonant timbre that could lift the spirits of a kingdom and bring comfort to those who sought his counsel.

"Oh, Freya," Calem said, putting his fork down. "I collected some spore samples for you. I hope they'll help you with your work."

"Thank you, that will be of utmost help," she replied, cheerfully.

As the twilight hues painted the sky in shades of deep violet and dusky blue, our royal family dinner came to a satisfying conclusion. Around the grand table, laughter and contented sighs lingered in the air, a testament to the joy shared in each morsel of the meal. Only bare bones remained of the once radiant roast duck, the heart of our feast. The once-fluffy mashed potatoes now lay as mere specks on the exquisite plate. The expansive salad bowl, previously brimming with a lush forest of lettuce leaves, held only a scattering of loose greens. All that remained was the sweet yet bitter elvenberry juice, a drink as enchanting as the tales spun in the twilight hours. The table, once a mosaic of flavors and textures, had been picked clean. The wonderful evening dinner was a reflection of the bonds that united our family— a painting of shared moments, laughter, and the deep comfort found in each other's presence. As the stars began to twinkle in the velvet sky, the memory of this exquisite meal lingered, a reminder of the love and nourishment that extended far beyond the confines of the table.

The night exuded serenity, while the star-studded sky infused the air with a sense of tranquility. I had already retired to my room for the evening and prepared to relieve myself from the tedious tug-of-war between wake and slumber when I heard a gentle knock on my wooden bedroom door.

"You may enter," I called out as I sat on the light fluffy comforter laid spread along my bed.

Reed drowsily stepped into my room and sat beside me.

"When would you like me to help you with your cooking lessons? You haven't made me aware of your schedule yet," he spoke softly and rubbed his tired eyes.

"Well," I spoke as I tried to collect my fatigued mind to recall my schedule, "I have dancing lessons with Freya tomorrow morning beneath The Weeping Willow's branches and right after that, I have a writers' workshop with my friend, Maia. I shouldn't be too busy at noon."

Reed nodded and said, "Noon works perfectly for me. I will meet you outside the first-floor kitchen."

"Thank you, Reed." I smiled before pulling him in for a tight hug. His dry tan skin felt rough against mine, but it felt nice to receive a hug nonetheless.

"By the way, your hair looks really beautiful tonight. I'm so used to seeing it pulled up," Reed grinned, "but it suits you. I'm surprised you have yet to find a handsome young man."

My cheeks flushed with heat, taking on a vivid hue of cherry red in response to those words. "I-I… Um- I don't really need a man at the moment."

He laughed, ruffling my hair. "I suppose my busy bee wouldn't have the time for something like romance, hm?"

I laughed as well, ducking away from his teasing hand. "I have a busy day tomorrow," I said, yawning. "I really should get some rest."

He smiled and nodded. "Sleep well, bumble bee." Once he had softly pulled my bedroom door shut, I let my weary body collapse and flop onto my bed.

Pondering the day to come, I mumbled, "I hope something interesting happens tomorrow. Don't you wish that too, Dew?" I tightly embraced my leaf-green teddy bear as I spoke to it. My heart longed for adventure, and the unknown no longer scared me. I *craved* it, a thirst for new horizons and uncharted territories that had grown insatiable. Day after day, the monotony of my life weighed upon me, casting a shadow over the once-glimmering potential of my royal existence. Life as a princess came with its multitude of duties, each one demanding unwavering attention and consuming the light of day, often spilling into the inky hours of the night. The collage of my routine, woven with obligations and responsibilities, had begun to feel like a gilded cage, confining me to a world that lacked the vibrancy and spontaneity that my spirit yearned for.

"I just wish something, *anything*, different would happen," I spoke to myself as a wave of sorrow rolled over me. "I just want some freedom…" My eyelids grew heavier and heavier until I couldn't control them and drifted off to sleep.

CHAPTER

2

As the first rays of dawn gently filtered through the lush canopy of trees, painting patterns on the floor of my room, I stirred reluctantly beneath my soft blankets. The morning's call seemed distant and uninviting as if the world beyond my bed was a realm I was not yet prepared to enter. My usually vibrant azure eyes were veiled by a heavy curtain of grogginess, my usual enthusiasm muted by the lingering embrace of sleep. Every limb felt as if it were wrapped in lead, and the thought of leaving the warmth and comfort of my cocoon-like bed was an arduous task. The melodious songs of birds, which usually ushered in the day with a sense of magic and wonder, now seemed like an intrusive symphony penetrating my drowsy consciousness. Inwardly, I wrestled with the internal debate between the allure of more sleep and the knowledge that the responsibilities of the day awaited me.

Suddenly a bright and brilliant idea flashed within my mind, causing a grin to creep onto my face. As the sun continued to rise above the treetops of our woodland home, casting a warm orange hue across the elven village, my playful smirk sparkled with mischief. With a sly twinkle in my eyes, I hatched a plan to infuse the mundane chore of gathering water for the luscious zen garden within the backyard of my home with a bit of sibling silliness. Calem had always been the more playful of my brothers, but I relished any chance to draw a precious laugh from him nonetheless. Slipping out my second-story window with the help of a study vine I conjured, I escaped my room and ventured into the forest to collect water from the freshwater stream that flowed nearby. With a full bucket and anticipation for the renewal of the traditional sibling prank wars, I quickly snuck back home. After I made it back into the safety of my room, I snuck down the hall to Calem's room. As I stood on a stool just outside his bedroom door, I carefully balanced the bucket above, securing it with a simple knot. I envisioned his reaction, shock followed by exasperation, and it filled me with excited anticipation. With one final adjustment, I stepped away, waiting for the inevitable moment when he would unknowingly spring my trap. The thought of his expression, the playful annoyance that would spark in his canary yellow eyes, brought a radiant smile to my face. Satisfied with my handiwork, I began my morning chores, humming a light tune under my breath, the thrill of the upcoming prank adding an extra skip to my step.

The sound of groggy footsteps snapped my focus to the practical joke that was about to take place. I swiftly got into position and waited patiently as excitement began to erupt from my being. With the turn of the door handle and a gentle push of the door, my plan was set into motion.

"Ilana! Seriously?!" Calem yelled as the crisp water soaked his silky sleepwear.

"Oops, did I forget to mention the new "welcome home" tradition?" I teased, giggling at his predicament.

Calem rolled his eyes as he spoke, "I can't believe I fell for that again."

"Reminds you of when we were younger, doesn't it?"

"Yeah, yeah, yeah," Calem responded, agitatedly.

"Well, at least you're hydrated now!" I giggled as he playfully ruffled my hair, uncaring about the new dampness on my scalp.

"Yeah, yeah. Just wait until you least expect it," he countered deviously.

"Oh, I'll be ready, big brother. And with glitter next time!"

"Glitter? That's crossing the line!" Calem exclaimed, bewildered by the words that escaped my mouth.

"Relax, it'll be magical!" I retorted as I lightly punched his shoulder playfully.

With a playful roll of his eyes that carried a hint of exasperated affection, Calem hobbled down the stairs, his steps slow but purposeful. I was aware that he knew that my antics were an integral part of our shared dynamic, a lighthearted dance that wove laughter into the fabric of our sibling bond. As he descended out of my sight, he turned his head briefly to face me and his lips curved into a half-smile, his heart warmed by the familiar ritual. The morning light streamed in through the windows, casting gentle shadows that seemed to echo the playful sparkle in his eyes. Without another word, he disappeared down the staircase of our home.

Without another moment of hesitation, I continued my daily routine. My footsteps, soft as whispers, carried me from room to room, as I delved into the familiar rhythm of my indoor chores. I paused by a window, my eyes momentarily drawn to the world outside, where the swaying trees seemed to beckon with promises of adventure and mystery. Yet, duty held me in its embrace, guiding me back to the tasks that had become the backdrop of my life. Dusting delicate trinkets and curios, I marveled at how the play of light on their surfaces conjured memories of ancient tales and shared laughter. The room exhaled a sigh of history, woven into its very fibers, a testament to the passage of generations. Slowly meandering down the stairs I greeted my parents before resuming my daily routine. Crossing into the kitchen, my fingers danced along the smooth surfaces of utensils and vessels, each imbued with a story of sustenance and communion. With practiced grace, I prepared a morning snack that bore the flavors of tradition, the aroma infusing the air with a sense of comfort and belonging. Moving to the small library within my home, shelves laden with tomes and scrolls, I ran my fingers over the well-worn spines, a silent acknowledgment of knowledge passed down through the ages. Dust motes floated in the warm beams of sunlight, like tiny echoes of those who had come before. My tranquil heart carried a deep reverence for the history ingrained in these walls, even as my mind wandered occasionally to the world beyond, yearning for the unknown. Each task, seemingly mundane, was a thread that connected me to the web of my heritage, weaving myself into the tapestry of my people's existence. And so, I moved through the house, chore after chore, embracing the ordinary as a conduit to the extraordinary, finding a symphony of solace in the seemingly repetitive notes of daily life.

After a seemingly endless hour and a half of chores and cleaning, I hastily made my way to our Great Willow Tree, knowing that my tardiness wouldn't go unnoticed.

"You're late," Freya said as she glanced at her timepiece.

"I'm sorry," I replied, breathless. "I was running a bit behind schedule this morning. Can we begin?"

"Of course," she spoke with enthusiasm as she nudged me and began her stretching routine.

My sister was a better dancer than I was. She looked so elegant and her movements seemed effortless, flawless. I, however, stumbled and fell, lacking the same grace she found with ease. Freya would joke around with me because of my clumsiness and I too would laugh, acknowledging my foible.

"You look like a headless chicken trying to do the hokey pokey," she laughed while she walked over to guide my movements.

"I'm doing my best here," I whined as she gently pulled my arm forward causing my shoulder to rotate fully and extend.

"You have to feel the energy flowing through you with every movement," Freya instructed. "The art of dancing is the key to unlocking your druid magic, Ilana. Don't forget that."

"I know, I know. I'll try harder-" I started, but she cut me off.

"No, I think you are trying too hard. Let it come naturally to you, it's in your blood."

I took a deep breath before beginning the routine once more. I allowed my eyes to drift shut as I focused on the feelings around me. I felt the soft soil beneath my rough bare feet and the pure natural energy flowing from the Great Willow Tree into its roots and then into myself from the soil. I felt tranquil for the first time in months as I moved fluently until I felt an unknown presence northern of our sacred tree. The energy emanating from its source felt determined and focused, but despite that, I also felt a strange kindness and warmth from it. Curiosity took control of my mind as I wondered who or what might be lurking nearby. My focus broke and I stumbled over my own feet and collapsed onto the ground, dashing any hope I may have dared accumulate of unraveling the chains that bound my druid magic.

"Ilana! Are you okay?" Freya ran over to me, tending to my mulberry-colored blood-smeared knee.

"I am alright. I think I'm just a bit exhausted that's all," I lied as I decided it would be best to keep my findings to myself in hopes of exploration and adventure.

"Let us take a break for today. It is going to be half impossible for you to dance with an injured knee like that." Freya almost looked disappointed in me, it made my heart sink deep into my chest. To dance the dance of druids, total concentration is required. To lose that concentration meant to lose fluidity and to lose all magic that had seeped into the body.

"Hey, Freya?"

"Yes? What is it?" she perked up, ready to listen to what I had to say.

"Thank you for attempting to teach me. I'll get it soon, I just know it." I paused and took a deep breath. "Could you tell Brother Reed that I won't be able to make it to my cooking lesson at noon? I just remembered that I had pre-planned events with Galadhwen."

"Of course," she replied with a kind smile before turning her back to me to continue her graceful dance.

I started towards the houses before ducking out of sight and sprinting into the northern forest. In the back of my mind, the fear of danger was screaming out to me, but I did not care. My mind was set on finding the source of the energy no matter what dangers it brought along with it. My heart was racing with excitement and anxiety for the first time in what felt like forever. This was the moment I had been waiting for, the adventure I had been wishing for, and the excitement I had been yearning for.

The prospect of stepping beyond the confines of my royal title and embarking on a journey into the unknown was both exhilarating and liberating. It was a chance to break free from the shackles of routine, cast aside the veil of privilege, and immerse myself in a world where I could truly discover who I was beyond the trappings of my birthright. The flutter of anticipation that stirred within me was like a caged bird finally tasting the winds of freedom, its wings unfurling with a newfound sense of purpose.

As I stood on the precipice of this new chapter, I felt a surge of determination coursing through my veins, propelling me forward with an unwavering resolve to embrace whatever challenges and wonders lay ahead.

The crisp air whipped past me as I continued to run in the direction of the presence I had felt before, eager to find its source until I suddenly felt the sharp presence of magic and stopped dead in my tracks. That's when I saw him.

In front of me, past a row of trees, sat a human boy, completely absorbed in his surroundings, his presence a stark contrast to the realm I had always known. He seemed to exist in harmony with the very environment that surrounded him, a testament to a world I had only dreamed of.

As I cautiously approached, I caught glimpses of his sketches taking form, each stroke of his pencil capturing the essence of the world he saw. His presence felt both foreign and strangely familiar, a reminder that adventure often comes in the form of unexpected encounters. I quickly ducked behind a tree in fear that he would see me. I felt his gaze fall upon the tree which I was shielded by.

"Who's there?" he demanded with a strange accent I couldn't recognize, "I know you are hiding. Come out peacefully and let's talk."

I was frozen, both in fear and enchantment. My heart raced like a wild creature, torn between the safety of familiarity and the intoxicating allure of the unknown. The prospect of crossing paths with this enigmatic human filled me with a sense of trepidation, as the lines between our worlds blurred in ways I had never imagined. Doubts and uncertainties swirled within me like a tempest, each gust of anxiety battling against the undercurrent of curiosity that tugged at my spirit.

And yet, despite the fear that threatened to hold me in place, there was an undeniable pull, an irresistible force that beckoned me forward. The allure of conversation, of sharing stories and perspectives that transcended our differences, was a siren's call that resonated deep within me. It was a moment poised on the precipice of transformation, where fear and anticipation mingled in a heady mixture, and the decision I made would inevitably shape the course of my adventure.

"Last chance to come out peacefully. I don't want to have to fight you." His voice went from firm to stern, and his hand was engulfed by blue electrical magic. The shrieking sound of the magic that he was conjuring was deafening. I snapped out of my daze and threw my body out from behind the tree, trembling in fear.

"Please don't hurt me, I'm not hostile!" I squealed and then my legs gave out and I collapsed to my knees. I was so terrified. Has my adventurous nature gotten the best of me? Had I, foolishly, waded too deep into trouble, unable to swim?

So many vivid thoughts crossed my mind, matching the speed of my heartbeat in a symphony of anticipation. The kaleidoscope of possibilities whirled through my head like a whirlwind, each scenario more vibrant and fantastical than the last.

What if our meeting led to an unbreakable bond, a friendship that transcended the boundaries of our worlds? Or perhaps our encounter would unravel misunderstandings and forge bridges of understanding between our people?

Even amidst these hopeful visions, the shadows of uncertainty loomed, reminding me of the potential risks and consequences. What if this encounter would end in my demise? The echo of my own heartbeat seemed to mirror the rhythm of my internal debate, a reminder that the choices we make in these moments of fleeting uncertainty have the power to shape our destinies in ways we may never foresee.

"Relax, I'm not going to hurt you. You just startled me, that's all." He spoke gently now, and the screaming of lightning subsided. He reached a hand down to assist me to my feet. "Are you ok? Did I hurt you?"

I noticed his gaze shift down to the wound on my knee, reopened now and sluggishly bleeding once again. He swiftly reached into his bag and revealed a white cloth that he began tying tightly around my knee to staunch the bleeding. I took his hand, allowing him to help me up, and said, "Th-thank you- um. What is your name?"

"Merlin, my name is Merlin." He smiled, "And you? What is your name, miss?"

"My name is Ila-" Pausing in contemplation, a flicker of doubt brushed against my thoughts, suggesting that perhaps revealing my identity as the elvish princess might not be the wisest course of action. The intricacies of his character and his intentions remained shrouded in mystery, a truth that pricked at the edges of my caution.

"Your name is Ila?" He asked confusedly.

"No, no, it's... um." I paused, considering my options.

"My name is Lala," I said quietly, "It is a pleasure to meet you."

"The pleasure is mine m'lady." He bowed to signify maturity and sophistication. I giggled a little at his enchanting behavior and closely observed him as I had not seen a human before. He quickly caught onto this because his face went from kind to puzzled.

"Why are you looking at me like that?" His eyes widened as he finally noticed my ears, "You're not human, are you? Ah, I understand." He smirked, and his voice took on a tone of mischief. "This must be the first time you have encountered a human as handsome as I."

"Actually I haven't ever seen a human at all. I've only heard stories about the destructive nature of your kind."

His eyes narrowed a little before he burst into laughter, "My kind? Destructive nature? You really haven't met a human before-"

"Then why don't you teach me?" I interrupted, eagerly.

"Pardon? You want me to teach you? How do you suppose I do that?" His evergreen eyes twinkled as he spoke, illuminating the same adventurous gleam that I had felt.

"Maybe I could, um, accompany you? Only for a little while so that I can understand?" I asked shortly before realizing how immature and naive I sounded. My lust for adventure had gotten the best of me and the silent screaming of reason had almost completely drowned out. "I'm sorry. I sound so foolish right now, don't I?"

He chuckled at my eagerness and replied, "Not at all. There is nothing wrong with wanting a bit of action in one's life."

I nodded and smiled, awaiting his instructions on what to do next. As he turned away from me to glance at his map, his chocolate brown hair shimmered in the various beams of light that poked through the thick cover of trees.

"Alright, Lala, come look at my map if you would please. Oh, and could you hold this right side up for me?" Merlin asked while he motioned for me to stand next to him.

While we cradled the map, his finger tapped on a radiant star, its brilliance labeled "Camelot", and then traveled with a purpose to a distant circle nestled in the southeastern expanse, marking a point far removed from its stellar guidepost.

"The star is my destination, and this circle here is where we are. It will be a long and arduous journey. Are you certain this is what you want?" He raised his left eyebrow.

"Of course. I wouldn't join you if I wasn't," I said with an eager grin.

"Where are your parents? Would you like to grab anything before we leave? I could walk you back-" he asked, but I cut him off.

"NO- I mean, no. We can just start heading to this Camelot place. I don't need anything nor do I need to tell anyone anything." My hasty response left him visibly puzzled and I quickly added, "I live out here alone and I always have. Let's not dwell on it."

"Alright," he said with a sigh and a shrug, "best be off then."

He gently folded his map, placing it into the tawny messenger bag that lay over his navy tailcoat. He set off northwest, his footsteps were purposeful and assured, and I quickly fell into step behind him, a heady rush of exhilaration coursing through my veins as I embarked on the unknown journey ahead. The spark of anticipation that had kindled within me now burned bright, igniting every sense with the promise of discovery.

With each step, the verdant landscape seemed to unfold like a tapestry of uncharted territory, and the scent of nature's essence, carried on the gentle breeze, stirred the air with the breath of unexplored frontiers. My heart pulsed with a mixture of anxiety and enthusiasm, a symphony of emotions that mirrored the alternating path before us—sometimes meandering through the whispering trees, other times darting across open clearings. The sun cast shifting patterns of light and shadow upon the earth, a metaphor for the journey that was both bright with hope and shadowed by the uncertainties that inevitably accompany the path of the untraveled.

My eyes were drawn to my companion's back, the straight line of his posture a reflection of his determination, a guiding beacon in a terrain that was both enchanting and mysterious. The rhythmic crunch of our footsteps on the forest floor was a harmonious backdrop to the symphony of nature's melodies—the rustle of leaves, the distant trill of a bird, and the murmur of a nearby stream.

With every stride, I felt a bond with the land strengthen, a connection that transcended the boundaries of my past life and intertwined my destiny with this newfound adventure.

The shadows of doubt that had once tugged at my thoughts began to recede, replaced by a resilient courage that spurred me forward. The landscape, once unexplored, was now etched with the imprints of our passage, an indelible mark on the canvas of our shared experience. As we ventured onward, I found myself yearning to drink deeply from the cup of the unknown, ready to embrace the trials and triumphs that awaited us beyond the horizon.

CHAPTER

3

Ad meliora, or, as the humans know it, "Towards better things". This saying circled within my mind countless times as we continued tramping through the thick vegetation of the forest. Sweat streamed down my face and back as the heat of the day exceeded my expectations, leaving me nauseous and dehydrated. Merlin was experiencing it too, despite his efforts to hide it. We rested for a few moments to saturate our dry mouths before continuing our pilgrimage.

"Merlin, maybe we should rest a bit. It is incredibly hot outside and it isn't good to get even more dehydrated than we already are." I said through gasping breaths, my heart racing for a whole new reason now.

"I asked you if you could handle this, Lala," he retorted, "We aren't stopping. This part of the woods isn't safe, especially after dark. Trust me, I would know."

"Can we… Could we at least make conversation?"

"No. It is best not to draw attention to ourselves here. In another few hours, we should be in the clear." His voice had lost its harshness, smoothing over my nerves.

I sighed but continued to trail behind him in silence, my steps occasionally stumbling over unseen roots and uneven terrain. Awkwardness lingered like a faint shadow around us, a reminder of the unfamiliarity that colored our interaction. The silence between us was punctuated only by the rustle of leaves underfoot and the distant chatter of unseen creatures.

As we pressed deeper into the woods, the density of the trees seemed to close in around us, creating an almost impenetrable barrier that further secluded us from the outside world. The canopy above obscured the sky, and the speckles of sunlight were muted to a mere glimmer, casting a dusky ambiance over our surroundings. It was as if we had entered a realm where time stood still, where the rules of the ordinary world held little sway.

The gradually encroaching darkness added to the sense of surrealism that enveloped our journey. With each step, the sparse sunlight dimmed further, and the forest's silence deepened, punctuated by the occasional whisper of a breeze through the leaves. The path we tread became a thread connecting us to the heart of the unknown, a journey that was both an exploration of the external world and an inner exploration of the self. As we ventured onward, the convergence of silence, darkness, and the subtle symphony of nature's echoes created an atmosphere of anticipation, leaving us poised on the cusp of a realm where anything was possible. I glanced at Merlin who seemed to have slowed down from the change in brightness. Although this eerie darkened atmosphere impacted Merlin, it did not have the same effect on me, thanks to the shadowsight possessed by the elvish race. As we journeyed further into the depths of the woods, the shroud of darkness that enveloped us held a different significance for me. The veil of night, while seemingly impenetrable to human eyes, was rendered translucent by my unique ability to perceive even the subtlest of shadows. The intricate dance between light and dark was a tapestry of nuances that I could discern, casting the forest in a mosaic that danced before my eyes.

The forest, cloaked in shadows, became an intricate web of shades and highlights for me. The inky expanse overhead was pierced by faint glimmers, hinting at the stars above. The shapes of trees and foliage took on a newfound clarity, each contour etched with a radiant luminescence that painted the scene in ethereal beauty. The play of light against the velvety backdrop allowed me to navigate the terrain with a sense of confidence that was otherwise unattainable in this shadowed realm.

As Merlin moved through the darkness with a sense of uncertainty, I felt a surge of gratitude for the gift bestowed upon me by my lineage. Shadowsight was more than just a physical ability; it was a reminder of the resilience and adaptability that defined our race. In the midst of this mysterious journey, my shadowsight was a source of solace, a guiding beacon that illuminated the path ahead and allowed me to experience the forest in a way that was both magical and deeply resonant.

Not only did the visibility change, but the temperature dropped dramatically as well which caused me to shiver. The forest's embrace had turned icy as if the very air itself had grown colder in response to the encroaching shadows. Despite the chill settled in my bones, a sense of exhilaration continued to course through me, spurred on by the adventure that had captured my heart and soul. Merlin glanced at me worriedly, but I waved off his concern. He nodded, then took hold of my arm for guidance.

Shortly after, the silence was consumed by the swelling orchestra of nocturnal critters that were crawling around our feet. My heart filled with warmth and awe, listening to the beautiful symphony of the dimly lit forest. Merlin seemed to notice my reaction, chuckling softly.

"Merlin?" I whispered.

"Yes?"

"I just wanted to thank you for allowing me to travel with you," I said gratefully with a smile.

"There is no need to thank me. I find it peaceful traveling alone, however, solitude can be the deadliest poison-" He paused, glanced at my expression, no doubt a touch blank with confusion, then started again, "I wanted some company. You aren't the only one getting something out of this."

"Could we stop and rest?" I dared ask. "It seems so peaceful here and the insects grace our ears with their unique songs."

"I already told you," he says, and the hesitant smile I had barely noticed slipped from my face, "it isn't safe here. We are almost outside the perimeter of the danger zone. Can't you just be patient?" With a scoff, he looked away from me.

"I…" Suddenly, I sensed a vague presence approaching us. It was faint as if it was being masked by something. I froze, then whipped around, holding up my hands, preparing to defend us.

"Lala, what's wrong?" Merlin yelled clearly startled by my sudden behavior, disturbing my concentration. His hands became enveloped by blue electricity and his stance changed as if he felt the same presence I had noticed moments earlier.

A sudden burst of force penetrated the ground below me, tightly gripping my ankle. A smokescreen of dust fell over the area, and I felt a firm bony hand jerk me downward into the earth. I screamed, but it quickly dissolved into a coughing fit. Dust coated thickly in my lungs, causing me to gasp desperately for air. My heart was pounding in my ears, a rhythmic drumbeat that echoed in the caverns of my chest. Adrenaline coursed through my veins, sharpening my senses to a needlepoint. In an instant, my world tilted, and the ground beneath me gave way as if the very earth sought to devour me. The taste of dirt was sudden, a gritty intrusion I choked on as I gasped for already sparse air. My mind raced, but it could do nothing to save me. All I could do was scramble for something, anything to save me, but my grasping hands only found more dirt, sliding uselessly between my fingers. I clawed at it, desperate and terrified, but I only continued to sink.

Seconds burned as an eternity as I struggled fruitlessly. The dirt only climbed, and my attempt to keep my head above the hungering earth, stretching my neck out, was meaningless. Only my hands remained above ground, still grasping even as my mouth filled with dirt. My lungs burned for air, but even if there was any, the pressure was too great for me to breathe.

As my consciousness blackened, I felt a rough hand grasp my own. I clung to it, desperate to escape, to live.

It was in vain. The hand, which was no doubt Merlin's, slipped away, transient as the dirt before it. I ached and despaired. For all the hopes I had built, the dreams of adventure, they all came to this. Dying, suffocating meaninglessly on the earth, with no idea as to why.

Just as I had come to accept my death, electricity jolted through me. My vision went white, and I was barely aware as the earthen maw clamped down on me loosened, and my limp body was pulled free. The air choked me as it revived my tarnished lungs, a bitter-sweet influx that carried both the promise of life and the lingering taste of near-death. Each gasp was a consonance of relief and agony, a reminder of the fragility of existence and the resilience of the spirit. As oxygen flooded my bloodstream, a rush of sensations accompanied its arrival— a heady mix of dizziness and clarity, of the ethereal sensation of life's thread being woven back into the fabric of my being. The contrast between suffocation and rejuvenation was a poignant reminder of the delicate balance that defines our mortality, a constant dance between the abyss and the light. As I drew in those precious breaths, I was acutely aware of the renewed vitality surging through me, a powerful testament to the unyielding strength that resides within us, even in the face of the most dire circumstances. I opened my soil-coated eyes while my body forcefully expelled the contaminates I had inhaled moments earlier. Meanwhile, the sound of electricity once more pierced my ears and a jolt of lightning shook the earth around me. My tear-filled vision identified a figure standing over me with an object clutched to its chest. *Merlin!* He shouted as he flung himself forward, releasing a screaming ball of blue magic from the palm of his hand. The forest was illuminated, blinding my recovering eyes and then there was nothing. No sound, no tugging, nothing. As I opened my eyes once more I saw Merlin panting, standing upright over me with his spellbook in hand.

"Are you alright?" he huffed while kneeling down beside me.

"I'm fine-" I coughed, "What was that?"

"I warned you that this forest was not safe," he reminded, firm but not unsympathetic. "It is home to the forest goblins. They don't take kindly to intruders marching about on their turf." Even as he scolded me, he glanced around for further danger.

"I'm sorry..." I whimpered, ashamed of my foolishness.

He rose to his feet, glancing at me. He hesitated, glancing at me. The moment stretched too long for my liking before he finally held out his hand. "Can you stand?" Offended by his words, I smacked away his hand.

"I can get up on my own. I don't need your *pity*." I spit the words from my tongue as if they had left a foul taste in my mouth and began stumbling northwest. My legs were unsteady. He was right, damn him.

"Wait, Lala." The actual regret in his voice was the only reason I stopped. "I'm sorry. I didn't… I am grateful for your company. I am, but I am also in a hurry. You've been nothing but kind, and I've been naught but a buffoon." We locked eyes, and he looked genuinely apologetic. "Could you forgive me?"

"I will accept your apology. I'm not as weak as I look, and I despise being treated as incapable." I felt a boulder of sorrow crushing me, the weight of it almost tangible against my chest, and a vivid memory flashed into my mind. I remembered, with a clarity that was both painful and cathartic, how as a child I was always looked upon as weak and frail because I was the youngest female-born royal elf. The memory was woven with the threads of sidelong glances and hushed whispers, innumerable unspoken expectations that had been thrust upon me. The mantle of my royal lineage weighed with the burden of preconceived notions, the belief that my stature made me inherently fragile, unable to endure the rigors that others could. It had bored itself into my sense of self, leaving me with the ever-nagging thought that maybe, just maybe, they were right.

As I stood motionlessly with my hand resting softly upon my bicep, the remnants of that memory played out in my mind like a silent film. The echoes of those old judgments reverberated within me, a symphony of doubt and insecurity that cast long shadows over my present circumstances. The sensation of being trapped beneath the earth seemed to echo the limitations that had once been imposed upon me, a poignant metaphor for the struggles I had faced in both the physical and emotional realms. I remembered sorrowfully how my activities were limited and I was constantly scolded by my father for my bashful behavior.

A sudden gentle hand rubbing my shoulder snapped me out of my daze. Merlin's glimmering eyes, peering directly into mine, were full of remorse and kindness. I felt my face get hot and I bit the inside of my cheek.

"Everything will be alright," Merlin soothed. "We should move just fifty more meters and we will be safe to rest for the night."

I nodded, weary, then asked, "How far is that in feet?"

Merlin glanced at me. Something he saw made him chuckle. "It's about a hundred fifty feet."

"Oh. That sounds... doable."

He laughed, and we started, once more, towards Camelot.

As time progressed, the sun began to fall into its routine slumber announcing the night's arrival. The insects exchanged places, their symphony of chirps and trills a vibrant testament to the shifting of time and the emergence of a new phase in the forest's nocturnal life. As the shadows cast by the trees began to stretch and blend, the once-thick canopy above gradually thinned, allowing more light to filter through, illuminating the surroundings with a gentle, mellow glow. It was as if the forest itself was awakening from slumber, transitioning from the cocoon of darkness to a realm where the boundaries between light and shadow merged into a captivating dance. The songs of the creatures—whispering crickets and murmuring frogs—filled the air with a sense of continuity, a reminder that life persisted in its myriad forms, even as the world underwent its cyclic transformations.

After Merlin had deemed it safe, we began to establish a secure campsite to await the sun's return. Merlin embarked on a mission to gather firewood, ensuring that the impending crisp evening would find us warmed by a crackling blaze. Meanwhile, I set to work fashioning a comfortable haven, crafting a resting place that promised us peaceful slumber and security throughout the night. I took a deep breath and began harnessing the druid magic that lay deep within me. I sensed the energy coursing beneath my feet, infusing my veins with its vitality as I commenced my druidic dance. I allowed my eyes to drift close, but strangely enough, I could see everything. The greenery surrounding me transformed into a dense cushion, ready to be spread beneath us, while a formidable barrier of thorny vines delineated the boundaries of our camp. I fluidly drifted my arms to the right to create a protective circle around the intended spot which we would generate a flame.

"Wow. You are *incredible!*" a familiar voice called out from behind me, breaking my concentration. I noticed with some embarrassment that a few of the new blooms drooped and wilted without my magic.

"Thank you. I can only perform druid magic with total concentration," I replied softly, my face warm and my head turned so I would not need to make eye contact. "I have not been able to master controlling my focus so my magic is still that of a novice."

Merlin carefully lowered the dry wood into the center of the barrier I had created and with a snap of his fingers, the wood was set ablaze. I carefully sat down so as to not ruin my filthy dress further and extended my arms so that my hands would feel the warmth of the fire. Merlin perched next to me and rustled through his bag before removing two angel-winged fish carefully wrapped in freshly gathered leaves from an elephant's ear plant.

"Wow, you truly were busy out there," I commented as I watched him work.

"Food is very important for the body and the mind," he responded, impaling our dinner on makeshift sticks and suspending them over the flames to ensure their thorough cooking.

"I have a question. And you don't have to answer if you do not wish to" I spoke vigilantly, watching his expression. "Why is it that you wish to go to this Camelot place marked on your map?"

His face fell and tensed. He slowly lowered his head and said, "My sister is very sick and needs me back at home, and I am her only hope for survival. I know of a possible cure for her ailment. I'm the only sorcerer that is strong enough to perform the sacred spell."

"I see." My voice softened, sympathetic. "I apologize for bringing such a topic up. I did not mean to cause you great sorrow."

"How could you have known?"

It didn't alleviate my guilt.

There was a long pause. We were equally as reluctant to speak in fear of distressing the other.

After an extended silence, Merlin spoke, "Let's change the subject, shall we? I want to know more about you since we will be traveling together for a long while. Besides, a beautiful creature like yourself surely has a story worth telling?"

"Oh no, not really." I answered quickly with an awkward laugh that fuelled the tension between us, "I don't have anything worth talking about."

Another uncomfortable silence wrapped around us, its presence echoing the unspoken thoughts and emotions that lingered in the air. The crackling of the fire seemed to underscore the weight of it, each flicker of flame casting shadows that mirrored the complexity of our unvoiced sentiments. It was as if the night itself held its breath, as though the world paused in anticipation of the thoughts that hovered on the edge of our tongues, waiting for the courage to find their voice. I felt my face turn flush as my eyes met his once more, but I quickly turned away from him, afraid that he would see my deepest secrets through them like windows.

"Is everything alright, m'lady?"

I nodded and my flustered face exceeded its usual shade of red. I felt the anxiety deep within my mind grow, its insistent tendrils weaving a web of unease that seemed to entangle even the most fleeting moments of respite. The crackling firelight that danced upon the edges of my vision offered a semblance of comfort, yet its warmth could not thaw the icy grip that anxiety had upon my thoughts. Each passing second carried with it the weight of unspoken words and unresolved emotions, the ever-present question of what lay ahead tugging at the fringes of my consciousness like an unwelcome companion. I realized that I didn't know how to maintain a proper conversation with Merlin since I had never been given the opportunity to try to communicate with humans. I grew quiet and shy, afraid of stringing together the wrong combination of words and offending him. The uncomfortable silence tensed with each second that passed, its weight pressing down upon us like a heavy shroud. We stood there, suspended in a quiet limbo, as if caught between the desire to bridge the gap of awkwardness and the fear of saying the wrong thing. It was as though the very air between us had thickened, the unspoken words reverberating with a palpable energy that seemed to echo the unexpressed thoughts that swirled within our minds. The moment hung like a fragile thread, a delicate balance between the yearning for connection and the vulnerability of exposing our innermost selves to the other.

"I'm sorry if I am behaving rudely. I've never gotten the chance to talk to a human before and I-" I started but was cut off.

"No, not at all. I haven't met a woman belonging to the wood elf race either. Apologies if my demeanor is uncomfortable as well."

"You have not offended me nor is your 'demeanor' uncomfortable." I reassured him, "I just don't know you quite yet and I am naturally introverted."

Merlin poked at the cooked fish, assuring that it was ready for consumption, before handing one to me and holding one for himself. I examined my meal, its aroma mingling with the earthy fragrance of the forest around us. The gentle crackle of the fire seemed to caress my ears, its rhythmic cadence a comforting backdrop to the ambiance of the night. The flickering dance of shadows cast by the flames painted an intricate canvas of movement, a silent symphony that played out in the corner of my vision. The cool touch of the evening breeze grazed my skin, carrying with it the whispers of stories untold and secrets buried beneath layers of foliage. At this moment, I felt a deep connection to the world around me, as if I were attuned to the very heartbeat of nature herself.

However, that changed when the fragrance of the fish grew so potent that it triggered a small sneeze to escape me, resulting in a hearty chuckle from Merlin.

"I hope its taste is better than its smell." Merlin joked before lightly jabbing me with his right elbow.

"Me too," I said laughing.

The silence returned to plague us while we ate our meals, the taste of the fish surprisingly sweet on my palate. Each bite was a revelation, the flavors melding in a way that was both unexpected and strangely satisfying. As we continued to eat in companionable silence, the interplay of taste and texture seemed to echo the nuances of our journey—full of surprises and uncharted territories. The fire's glow illuminated our makeshift campsite, casting a warm, flickering light that painted our surroundings in an otherworldly palette of shadows and highlights. It was a moment suspended in time, a pause in the midst of our adventure, where the simple act of sharing a meal spoke volumes in the language of camaraderie. I acknowledged my dearth of communication skills but lacked a solution to the problem. If Father had seen me this way, he would fear I had gone mad. I never before struggled to talk to others aside from my usual introverted personality. I wanted to talk to him, I just didn't know what caused sunken feelings of pain to pool within the recesses of my chest. The weight of unspoken words bore down upon me, like a heavy burden that whispered of missed opportunities and the ache of withheld emotions. It was as if the chasm between us was both physical and emotional, a barrier that seemed insurmountable in its complexity. As the night deepened around us, the yearning to bridge that gap mingled with the sting of unshed tears, an amalgamation of emotions that seemed to simmer just beneath the surface.

"Hey, I have an idea!" Merlin perked up as he spoke, seemingly enthusiastic. "We should play a game, to get to know each other."

"What do you suggest?" I questioned.

"Cleric's Truth seems like the obvious choice. Do you know it?" he asked as he tilted his head, allowing a thin veil of hair to mask his face.

I remembered an obscure memory of playing the mentioned game with fellow classmates at a young age. Cleric's Truth was a game with rather simple rules. One player would ask a question, then both players would have to answer it with the unequivocal truth. Both participants would also provide an explanation for their answers if applicable. If a player is unwilling to answer, they would have to do whatever the other player commands within reason. Either player is allowed to object to the command, thus ending the game. However, there's a catch. Whoever ends the game first has to pay a price hence the risk component of playing. This can vary between cooking a fine meal to buying an item of the other players' choosing.

"So, how about it? Would you grant me the honor of playing Cleric's Truth with me?" Merlin asked with a kind smile and a shimmer in his eyes.

"I would love to," I responded with a giggle due to his convincing charm.

I felt a feeling of warmth that I had believed I would never feel again: true happiness. It was as if a long-forgotten ember within me had been rekindled, casting its gentle glow upon the shadows that had clouded my heart. The beauty of the starry sky above and the crisp touch of the midnight breeze seemed to conspire, intertwining their soothing embrace to ease the anxieties that had gripped me earlier. Each twinkling star overhead felt like a reassuring presence, a reminder that the vast universe held secrets and mysteries beyond our comprehension. As the cool breeze brushed against my skin, carrying with it the whispers of far-off places and distant dreams, I felt a sense of solace settle within me, a respite from the tumultuous sea of emotions that had churned within my soul. The flickering of the blazing inferno before me granted a feeling of security and the crackling cleared my once hazy mind. Merlin's green eyes twinkled and his altruistic smile reassured me that I was where I was meant to be. I felt content, at peace, and I felt jubilant. I smiled at Merlin, positively overwhelmed by these robust emotions, and gently reached out in hopes of grasping his rough hand in mine. He gladly took my hand as we started our game.

"I'll go first, alright?"

I nodded and waited, patient but excited, for the question he was conjuring within his head.

"Let's start simple, what is your favorite color?" His words were playful and pure as he responded to the question he had asked, "Mine is a deep violet-blue."

"My favorite color is mint green, just like the dress I am wearing. This has been my favorite color since I could perceive them." I said in an attempt to follow the game's guidelines.

Merlin nodded, proving to me that I had his undivided attention.

It was my turn to ask a question, but I hadn't the slightest clue what to ask. The weight of uncertainty hung heavy in the air, a palpable reminder that the choice of words could shape the trajectory of our conversation and perhaps even our budding connection. The backdrop of the night, with its countless stars shimmering above us, seemed to mirror the infinite possibilities that stretched before me. As I grappled with the vastness of the universe and the confines of my own thoughts, I felt a mixture of vulnerability and determination stir within me. It was a moment that held both the potential for awkwardness and the promise of genuine understanding, a single query poised on the precipice of unlocking a world of shared experiences and newfound revelations. I thought back to my family and thought it best to ask him about his.

"What is your family life like?" I cautiously asked. I hadn't thought far enough to realize what a foolish idea that was.

"Ah, that's a complicated question. I will answer to the best of my ability." He responded, pondering the best possible method of answering. "I am the offspring of the king and queen of Camelot, Sir Arthur Grimald and Lady Morgan Grimald. I have two older brothers and an older sister. Their names are Vulcan Grimald, Talon Grimald, and Cerie Grimald. Our family had its imperfections of course, but we love each other very much."

I nodded and squeezed his hand tighter, "You must miss them very much. I will accompany you in finding your way back home, no matter what it takes, Prince Merlin."

He smiled in gratitude for my gesture. He asked, "What about your family? Remember, the rules of the game state that both players must answer."

My face fell, the weight of uncertainty settling over me like a shroud, and I felt the anxiety creep back in. It was as if the fragile thread of connection we had woven was fraying, and the fear of revealing too much threatened to pull it apart completely. I knew that the truth was a vulnerable path, one that could expose my innermost thoughts and desires, leaving me open to judgment, danger, and misunderstanding. And yet, the thought of lying to protect myself, of weaving a web of half-truths to shield my emotions, left a bitter taste in my mouth. It was a difficult choice to make, a conflict between the desire for authenticity and the instinct to safeguard my heart and my people. As the battle raged within me, I recognized that sometimes self-preservation required the art of deception, a skill that came at the cost of authenticity and weighed heavily on my conscience.

"I have no family. I never knew them either. All I remember is awakening in the forest amongst the plants." I fibbed and the feeling of sorrow crept back into my heart fearing the prolonged feeling of betrayal that Merlin would experience when the truth shines through the twisted web of lies.

"You are not alone now," Merlin said as he pulled me into a soft embrace. I felt my face grow warm, but no matter how nice it was, all I felt was shame. The embrace, though fleeting, was a brief respite from the sea of complexities that had enveloped us. It was a bittersweet moment of solace, where the walls between us seemed to momentarily crumble, and the shared embrace held the promise of connection. And yet, beneath the surface, the truth lingered—a truth I knew could not be avoided forever. It was a paradox of emotions, the warmth of the hug juxtaposed against the chill of impending honesty. As I held onto that fleeting moment, I wondered if perhaps vulnerability could be the key to unlocking the bridge between us, a bridge built on shared truths rather than the illusion of protection. Even though I wasn't alone as I had told him, I still felt it deep down and his generosity warmed my core.

"I-It's your turn," I said, stuttering.

"Ah, right," he replied, releasing me from the pleasant hug. "What is your biggest wish or dream?" His eyes pierced mine as if they were enchanted spears commanding my attention and refusing to allow my gaze to wander.

"I wish to live a peaceful life without the fear of violence. I want to be free of that fear so that I can experience the world, see it, explore it." I said, my eyes had drifted shut and my hands had come to rest over my heart. I found solace in that this, at least, was sincere. I felt bound by the chains my family threw upon me, that tethered me to my village. I wanted to explore ever since I was little, but I never got to because of my supposed royal duties. The weight of those unfulfilled desires had always rested heavily on my shoulders, a reminder of the path not taken and the dreams left behind. The lure of the unknown had always tugged at my spirit, beckoning me to venture beyond the confines of the palace walls and into the world that lay beyond. But the demands of my title had shackled me, their grip unyielding as I navigated the expectations placed upon me. The hunger for exploration had remained a persistent ember within me, a flicker of longing that refused to be extinguished. And now, as the opportunity for adventure presented itself in the form of this journey, the dormant flame blazed to life once more, threatening to consume my doubts and illuminate the path forward.

"Keep me around long enough and that will be an absolute," Merlin said with a wink. "As for me, I wish for a life free of demands and duties which I need to fulfill. I just want to be able to live my life. It's always "Merlin do this" and "Merlin do that". I just want to be able to do what *I* want to do".

My eyes widened as he spoke, the realization settling upon me like a gentle revelation—his dream was identical to my own. In that moment, a sense of kinship blossomed between us, a connection forged by shared desires and parallel aspirations. It was as if our souls had found a common rhythm, dancing to the same melody of longing and yearning. The weight of isolation that had once burdened me seemed to lift, replaced by a profound relief that I was not alone in the need for freedom and the thirst for exploration. As his words lingered in the air, a bridge seemed to form between our hearts, a bridge built upon the foundation of understanding and empathy. And in that bridge, I glimpsed the promise of a friendship that transcended the boundaries of our pasts and held the potential to shape our futures. At that moment there was no Merlin, but a caged bird that was trapped because it was needed for singing, however, its need to fly was ignored. In that moment I wished to unlock the cage of expectations to allow him to take flight to find his own path, hoping that he would do the same for me.

But I had lied to him. I had lied to him, and it was too late to change that. As it was, I couldn't let him know that was a dream we shared.

"Lala," a voice snapped me back to reality. "Have you ever wished you could just escape from this reality?"

Quietly, ashamed of myself, I whispered, "I have."

"Well, how about this? Let's forget about this world tonight and have fun. How does that sound?" Merlin asked as he stood up and reached his hand out to me.

I looked up at him, puzzled by his words. I asked, "What do you mean?"

"Well-" He began by snapping his fingers, conjuring three small mandolins, a pan flute, and several other instruments seemingly out of thin air. These exquisite magical instruments mirrored the radiant blue hue of Merlin's magical aura, levitating gracefully around us. With a synchronicity that bordered on the supernatural, they came to life, playing a captivating melody that resonated through the air, bouncing off the surrounding trees and filling the atmosphere with an entrancing rhythm. The songs they crafted seemed to pirouette about the rustling leaves, forging an enchanting symphony that spoke to the very essence of the forest. It was as if these instruments possessed a life of their own, their celestial melodies twirling through the air, enfolding us in an embrace of pure enchantment. In the midst of this magical serenade, a flicker of elation ignited within me—a vivid reminder that amid life's uncertainties and vulnerabilities, pockets of joy, connection, and shared wonder could still be found, transcending the ordinary and illuminating the path ahead.

"May I have this dance?" Merlin asked, bowing with one hand behind his back and the other held forward, an offering for me to take.

My face turned as red as a freshly picked tomato and I took his hand, and with it, his invitation.

I took a deep breath as we started, my heart quickening with a mixture of excitement and trepidation. The fear of embarrassing myself further loomed like a shadow, threatening to cast doubt on my abilities and disrupt the harmonious moment. With each note played and each beat followed, I focused on the rhythm, allowing the music to guide my movements and soothe my nerves. The enchanting melody seemed to envelop us, creating a cocoon of sound where my insecurities could momentarily fade into the background.

As we danced on, I became acutely aware of the bond that was forming between us, a connection forged through the shared experience of making music together. And with every note that resonated in the air, my confidence grew, the fear of embarrassment giving way to a sense of accomplishment that was both unexpected and deeply gratifying. At first the motions were simple to test each other's abilities, but gradually advanced in both speed and difficulty. A relaxing box step turned into a series of flamboyant twirls and flashy leg movements. My heart was pounding from the buzz of emotion and I let out a soft laugh. Merlin stared past my eyes and into my soul and reciprocated the laughter. I felt my brilliant azure irises twinkle as his captivating gaze continued to lock onto mine.

I felt his energy bond with mine with each touch as the dance continued. It was warm and smooth like newly spun silk, fluidly colliding against my eccentric waves of druid energy. In that moment, I felt unified with everything around me; the land, the trees, even Merlin himself. The music seemed to dissolve the boundaries that had once separated us, weaving a tapestry of connection that stretched beyond the physical realm. The vibrations of the instruments resonated not only within my body but also within the very fabric of the world, as if every note played echoed through the collective soul of nature itself. As the music flowed through us, I found myself immersed in a profound sense of belonging, a feeling that whispered of the profound interconnectedness that bound us all together in the grand dance of life. With each passing moment, the freedom I felt increased drastically. I was happy, and I never wanted to let go of that feeling. My heart had taken flight, sprouting wings to find the paradise it longed for.

Beat by beat, the melodies lifted me higher, carrying me away from the worries and constraints that had held me captive. The music along with Merlin's embrace was a vessel that carried me to a realm beyond the physical, where my spirit soared and danced alongside the ethereal strains. In that moment, I was no longer bound by the limitations of the world; instead, I was free to explore the vast expanse of my own imagination. The symphony reverberated through me, creating a bridge between the ordinary and the extraordinary, between the present and the dreams that had once seemed out of reach. It was as if this moment itself had become the key to unlock the hidden doorways of my heart, inviting me to embrace the paradise that had always existed within, waiting for the right melody to set it free.

The song had reached its coda, but I did not care. The moment held my mind hostage inside a soundproof room and I continued to smile, not recalling when I had started. Alas, a beautiful dance which had seemed endless concluded with a giant crescendo of sound and emotion. Our bodies halted at a tight, close-eyed embrace as the silence was welcomed back into the forest.

We said nothing for a while, still returning to reality along with its feats and flaws. The echoes of the music lingered in the air, their fading resonance a gentle reminder of the enchantment we had woven. As the last notes dissipated, the forest seemed to sigh in response, it's quiet embrace welcoming us back to reality. The transition was gentle yet palpable, like stepping from a beautiful dream into groggy wakefulness. The night held a hushed reverence, as if it too had been touched by the magic that had woven its threads through the air.

And as we found ourselves in the present moment once more, I sensed a newfound sense of closeness, a shared experience that transcended words and united us in the painting of our shared journey. I felt safe within his warm grasp and allowed myself to press into him, a subtle gesture that spoke volumes of the trust and connection that had blossomed between us. The embrace was more than a physical contact; it was a testament to the bond we had forged, a silent affirmation that even in the midst of uncertainty and vulnerability, we could find solace in each other's presence. The beat of his heart beneath my cheek seemed to sync with my own, creating a rhythmic symphony that resonated with the unspoken understanding that flowed between us. It was a moment suspended in time, where words were unnecessary, and the warmth of his embrace whispered promises of friendship, companionship, and the shared journey that awaited us. I could feel drowsiness descending onto me like a soft blanket. I wanted to remain in this drifting state for all eternity if it meant that his embrace would never release me.

Despite my wishes, all good things must come to an end and with that he ended the embrace, taking a few steps backwards. His eyes widened causing me to look around out of curiosity only to result with the same reaction. My jaw nearly dropped at the sight. How had I not seen it before this moment? Elegant plant structures reached towards the canopy, enveloping our campsite in their verdant embrace. Their endless whorls enthralled me. The structures matched the emotions and elegant freedom I had felt causing me to wonder if I had been the cause of their creation.

"Wow, that is just... so incredibly beautiful," Merlin had said in awe, turning to face me.

"Did I do this?" I asked in disbelief.

He nodded and walked around the perimeter, admiring each individual vine, flower, and leaf. I looked down at my hands, unable to grasp the power I had expelled.

"I hadn't been able to conjure this amount of energy before. How did I do it now?" I barely noticed I had said it aloud, I may not have had Merlin not answered me.

"Because you felt pure emotional happiness, Lala. This is your true power." Merlin responded, overhearing me as I talked to myself. He wrapped his left arm around me and smiled. My eyes stung, and I wasn't sure why until I felt tears cascade down my rosy cheeks. Slowly, Merlin's words sunk in. All my hard work and suffering actually paid off, culminating in a moment of triumph that had washed away the trials I had endured. The sense of accomplishment was as sweet as it was unexpected, a reminder that perseverance and dedication could yield results beyond what I had imagined. All of it has led to this. It truly was fate that guided me along this path of adventure. The happiness overwhelmed me as I sank to my knees and broke into sobs. Merlin put his gentle hand on my shoulder once more in an effort to soothe me. I had found the emotion I had been longing for my whole life. The feeling that consumed my mind and body was truly pure.

Minutes passed and my sobs subsided, leaving me with happiness and somnolence. I gathered that Merlin had felt the same from his poorly hidden yawns behind his kind smile. I ushered him to his thick mattress of soft plants and squishy moss before lumbering over to my own.

"These beds are incredible," Merlin said through yawns.

"Your admiration is much appreciated," I responded with the same drowsiness.

I glanced over at Merlin only to see that he had already dozed off, only minutes after lying down. I chuckled quietly to myself and waved my hand, creating a thick leaf blanket that rested upon Merlin's exposed body. I sat upon my makeshift bed and fluffed out my dress to limit the wrinkling. I twirled my right index finger to create a cocoon of greenery, sealing my bed and myself in an undisturbable environment. I smiled, resting my head and falling deeply to sleep.

CHAPTER 4

Amor est vitae essentia. "Love is the essence of life". What is love? How does one understand this emotion? How does one know they feel it? How do you behave when feeling this suffocating emotion? I had not known love. I understood the blood-related love that nearly every family in our colony had experienced, but not *this* emotion that has plagued my mind. Was it good or bad? Is it a strength or a weakness?

How was I to know that answer? These questions, these feelings, and these desires both intrigued me and terrified me. The more I pondered, the more I realized that love was a vast ocean of emotions, each wave carrying with it the potential for joy and pain, connection and vulnerability. It was a force that could elevate the soul to unprecedented heights or leave it shattered against the rocks of heartache.

I yearned to understand it, to decipher its intricacies and navigate its tumultuous currents, yet the uncertainty and fear held me back. What if I opened my heart only to find emptiness? What if the vulnerability it demanded proved to be my undoing? The paradox of love was a riddle I could not solve, its complexity a reflection of the human experience itself. And so, with a mixture of trepidation and curiosity, I embarked on a journey of self-discovery, determined to unravel the enigma of love and, in doing so, uncover the depths of my own heart.

I woke up with a gasp, drenched in sweat only to see the shining sun through my secured capsule.

"What… What was I dreaming about?? Was it a nightmare?" I asked myself, wiping my drenched forehead.

I lightly poked my earth-made coffin causing it to open up, squinting into the blinding light of the morning sun. The air felt fresh and clean, and the forest sparkled with glistening diamonds of morning dew. The delicate scent of earth and leaves filled my lungs, invigorating my senses and reminding me of the vitality that thrived in every corner of the natural realm. The symphony of bird calls harmonized with the gentle rustling of leaves, creating a chorus that serenaded the birth of a new day. In this pristine sanctuary, I found solace and a connection to the simple yet profound beauty that nature offered, a beauty soothed the restless yearnings that resided within me. I raised my arms to stretch out my sore back, the motion accompanied by a satisfying series of cracks and pops, momentarily relieving the tension that had accumulated. The stretch of my muscles and joints was like a small victory over the physical strain that came both with our journey and the activities of the previous night. As I lowered my arms, a sense of rejuvenation washed over me, a reminder that even amidst challenges and uncertainties, there were small moments of respite and renewal that could help restore both body and spirit. I had not danced at that level before and my body ached from it. I yawned before I glanced over to where Merlin had been sleeping, but he was nowhere to be seen. My drowsy mind filled with panic as I jumped to my feet, frantically calling out his name.

"Merlin? Merlin, where are you?" I cried out, but there was no response. I sprinted over to where he had slept, my heart pounding within my chest, only to notice that his belongings had disappeared.

The realization hit me like a lightning bolt, a surge of adrenaline coursing through my veins as panic and disbelief mingled within me. My heartbeat, once steady, now thundered in my ears, matching the rapid pace of my breaths. Thoughts raced through my once hazy mind, each one a fragmented puzzle piece that contributed to the growing sense of urgency and unease. It was as if the forest had conspired to swallow him whole, leaving behind only traces of his presence and the echoing void of his absence. The world around me seemed to blur as I grappled with his sudden disappearance. I shook my head against my catastrophizing, attempting to regain my rationality. Maybe he had gone for a morning walk? Maybe he had gone for food? But, why was all of his stuff missing? I couldn't take it anymore.

"MERLIN!"

I bent over, attempting to catch my breath as I gasped for air. Panic welled in my chest, a swirling tempest that threatened to overwhelm me. The forest, once a place of wonder, now felt dark and unknown, its once familiar beauty transformed into a labyrinth. As I struggled to steady my breathing, the knowledge that I was alone crept in. Alone, and directionless.

Merlin had the map.

My desperate scream echoed, causing birds to flee in fear, and a giant, razor-sharp thorn filled garden burst from the ground. In the silence that followed, I fell to the thorn-covered ground and sobbed. The echoes of my own sad little sounds mocked me.

I am alone.

As I wept, I felt the comfort and warmth of druidic plants wrap around me, and I curled into them just the same.

How could he have just left me there? Why? Did he really just leave, or was this some plot, the violence of humans he once denied coming now to devour me like the earth he had saved me from?

Such vile thoughts echoed in my mind. Even if he had simply abandoned me, what was I supposed to do? I was so far from home in the middle of nowhere, and I had only made it this far with his aid. I had no way of finding a way back to my home.

I was alone.

My father's voice resonated deep within my heart. In my moment of despair, the memory of his words, his guidance, and the strength he had instilled in me came rushing back, a lifeline of reassurance cutting through my tumultuous thoughts. In that moment, it was as if he was there, hugging me, offering solace and strength, even alone as I was. His wisdom echoed like a beacon in the darkness, reminding me that I was not alone, that the bond of love and connection could transcend the barriers of distance and time. It was a comforting reminder that, even in the face of uncertainty, the lessons and guidance imparted by those we hold dear can serve as a guiding light, leading us through the darkest of moments and anchoring us to the essence of who we are.

"To be alone and to feel alone are different, even if they seem the same. The person feeling alone feels deep sorrow, but their sanity, their "humanity" remains intact. One who is truly alone is no longer a person, but a being veiled in a thick darkness that has consumed even the dimmest light. And you, my dear, will never be alone. Not while you have your family." His soothing words resonated within me, it wrapped around my heart, and withered away the vicious throned vines of sorrow that had before. .

The weight of my isolation seemed to lift, replaced by a sense of connection that spanned the boundaries of time and space. His words were a balm for my wounded soul; reminded me that the love and guidance he had bestowed upon me were still present, still guiding me even in the midst of uncertainty. As his words settled within me, the tendrils of loneliness loosened their grip, and a spark of hope ignited within the darkness. I felt the warmth of my father's words swell in my chest before clutching my own body closer, seeking solace in the embrace of his memory and the protection he always gave. With each beat of my heart, I could almost hear his voice, a steady presence guiding me through the storm. The memory of his strength, his wisdom, and his unwavering support became a lifeline that anchored me in the present, offering a sense of security even in the face of the unknown. As I held onto his memory, I found the courage to face the challenges that lay ahead, knowing that his love was a constant, a beacon that could illuminate even the darkest of paths.

A sudden familiar voice startled me, dragging me back to the surface of reality's lake.

"Lala? Can you hear me?" Merlin yelled out, his voice muffled but concerned.

I opened my tightly closed eyes to see Merlin fighting through the thorny labyrinth that tore at his clothes and skin. I slowly reached out to him, hoping the sharp plants would disappear, but they did not. The magical plants I had conjured in my emotional distress couldn't be reversed. The walls I had built in fear no longer felt like safety, but I could not tear them down.

The frustration of my predicament gnawed at me. . The emotions that had surged within me, like a tempest, had left their mark on the world around me, an echo of my internal turmoil made manifest. This is why I was supposed to learn control.

"Merlin," I called out, my voice weak. "Merlin, stop. Let me come to you. I can't sit here and watch you get injured by my uncontrollable magic."

"No. It's okay, I'm coming, Lala." His hands tore up as he forced his way through the cruel thorns. "It'll all be okay."

I tried to do something, anything to ease the pain he would have to go through to work his way to me, but it was for naught, and I could do nothing but watch as he pressed his way, agonizingly slowly, through the twisted thorns, watch as he flinched at the small cuts they dug into his skin and the minute tears they dug into his clothes.

It felt like an eternity before he finally broke through, stumbling to me. Merlin spoke softly to soothe my worries, "I have you now, it'll be alright." He scooped me up before I could say a thing, then turned to the wall of thorns he had just navigated.

My heart beat against my chest as he returned to the thorns, and, without hesitating, he braved them once more, pushing them away from me, uncaring as they dug deeply into his skin.

All for me.

In an instant, had it really been so quick?, we were out. "What happened?" Merlin asked, gently setting me onto my feet.

"I-I thought you left me. I was so scared. I don't know." I looked down, not meeting his eyes. I couldn't bear the worry in them. "I'm sorry."

"Lala, listen." He grabbed my hands, tugging on them lightly until I looked back up at him. "I am not going to up and leave you here." I was only out hunting for food."

"But," I look away to the remains of our campsite. "But your stuff was gone, I had thought-" I trailed off.

His eyes sparked with realization when I looked back at him. "Ah. I had to bring it with me, to carry whatever it is I decided to bring back. I also needed my spell book so that I could easily strike down a source of meat and protein. I couldn't carry all of this in my two arms, you see?" Merlin said, motioning humorously with his arms, laughing lightly at his attempt to lighten the mood.

I took a deep breath to keep myself from crying again. I was truly embarrassed and wished to curl in a ball and cease to exist to end the torturous pain that came with the overwhelming weight of my emotions. The sensation I felt was a sharp blade that cut deep, leaving behind a mix of shame and frustration. I longed to escape the harsh glare of my own self-criticism, to find solace in the shadows and shield myself from the raw exposure of my feelings. My shame knotted deep in my chest.

"Hey, it's alright." He ducked his head, trying to meet my eyes. When I looked, he continued, "I just need you to *trust* me. Can you do that, please?"

I blushed and said, "Yes. I'm sorry. I trust you."

Trust is a very strong word. To trust or not to trust is a creature's willing choice. However, there is no in between. Either there is trust or there is not. It's that simple.

~~~

The sun kept rising, aiming to reach its peak to announce the arrival of the afternoon. It had been hours since we packed and left our first campsite to travel the slowly diminishing distance between my homeland and Camelot. The air felt cooler than the previous blistering day, a welcome respite from the oppressive heat that had surrounded us. Each breath I took seemed to cleanse my lungs, invigorating my senses and offering a renewed sense of vitality. The gentle breeze carried with it the scent of earth and foliage, harmony at work. The light breeze felt pleasant, combating the sun's heat to create weather's perfect balance. I glanced over at Merlin who was smiling at the sun's rays that were poking through the intermediate cover of trees. His peaceful smile bolstered a sweet grin that escaped from my curious face. I felt oddly enlightened when I was with him, something I hadn't felt before. I thought back on the circling questions that consumed my mind the night before, but shook my head with the determination to stay present.

"Hey, Lala?" Merlin called out before glancing over at me.

"Yes? What is it?"

"Have you thought about what you'll do when we reach Camelot?"

"Well I-" I trailed off only to shake my head and continue, "No I haven't."

Merlin chuckled a little and said, "We'll worry about it when we get there, then."

I smiled at him, but my thoughts didn't move on. I really had no plans aside from helping Merlin achieve his goal. The future stretched before us, an open canvas yet to be painted, and my own desires and ambitions paled in comparison to the urgency of the task at hand. The clarity of purpose was both reassuring and humbling. As I gazed into the horizon, I couldn't help but feel a commitment to stand by Merlin's side and face whatever challenges awaited us with unwavering resolve. And as our paths merged, the possibilities of the unknown unfurled before us, a shared destiny that held the promise of adventure, discovery, and the unbreakable bond that had woven us together.

As we continued to walk through the thinning forest, Merlin decided to dive nose deep into his spell book. He continued to play around with his lightning magic, making various strange zapping noises. I admired his magic. It was something I had never seen or studied, and it naturally captivated my attention. The flickering arcs of energy that danced from his fingertips held a mesmerizing beauty, each spark a testament to the power he wielded with such enviable ease. I watched as he shaped and controlled the elemental force, a symphony of light and sound that seemed to spring from the very core of his being. It was a reminder of the vastness of the magical world, where each individual possessed their own unique talents and abilities, a reminder that the threads of magic wove through every corner of our existence. As I observed him, a sense of awe settled over me, a silent tribute to the wonders of the unknown and the depth of the mysteries that awaited our discovery. My lack of surrounding awareness consequently caused me to trip and make a fool of myself. I regained my original stance before laughing alongside Merlin at my clumsiness.

"Hey Merlin, can we play a game while we walk?" I asked softly.

"I don't see why not. What do you propose?"

"Maybe… Never Have I Ever?"

"I have a better idea," Merlin said with a devious smirk. He suddenly threw his book into his bag before he spun around to face me. His arm shot towards me, and he tapped my arm. Laughing, he declared,, "Tag you're it!"

Before I could even react, he started rushing off in a clumsy hurry, twisting his way around the roots and branches in our path. I laughed and chased after him, slowly catching up and eventually tagging him. Merlin was laughing loudly as we played, all the while rushing us closer to our destination. His infectious laughter echoed through the forest, mixing together in harmony with the birdsong above. The energy of our shared playfulness was like a current that surged between us. With each chase and every burst of laughter, the weight of our worries seemed to lift, replaced by the simple pleasure of the present moment. The last time I had this much fun was when I was a kid during our break from druid practices. At this moment, both of us were children again, running around without a care in the world. The forest around us became a playground of possibilities, a canvas on which we could paint our laughter and shared moments of happiness. And as we chased each other through the foliage, the world transformed into a haven of pure innocence and spontaneity.

It's all fun, that is, until someone gets hurt. Merlin tripped, his foot catching as he stepped over a partially unearthed tree root. He yelped in pain as he fell to the ground, poorly cushioned by dried dead leaves, twigs and sharp pebbles.

"Merlin! Are you ok?" I rushed over to him before kneeling down beside him as he grasped his injured foot.

He groaned and winced in pain. "I think I twisted my ankle."

I closed my eyes to focus my magic into my hands. Thick leaves that I conjured, wrapped around Merlin's ankle, creating a bootlike protection around the wounded extremity.

"Don't you know elvish healing magic? Why not just heal my ankle?"

I shook my head, apologetic. "It's too risky. I haven't perfected it and I'm afraid of doing more harm than good." I responded wistfully.

He frowned and nodded. I'm certain he knew I wished I could do more, that he understood I knew he was in a rush. I just couldn't risk slowing us down even further with a botched healing.

"I'm sorry. This is all my fault. It was my idea, I shouldn't be slowing us down just for a little distraction."." I whimpered as the sight of his pain made my stomach turn.

"Don't blame yourself. These things happen from time to time." He responded, gritting his teeth in pain.

"At least we had a bit of fun," I said, joking and consoling in equal measure.

He half-smiled at me as he struggled to get back onto his feet, determined to keep going even still. The raw edges of his resilience were on display, his spirit refusing to waver. I wrapped his arm around my shoulder to provide him additional stability and we began slowly hobbling north.

Merlin would grimace occasionally as we pressed on, moving slower than ever due to his injury.

I felt horrible. I never meant for this to happen.

Merlin hadn't mentioned blaming me, but he hadn't said he didn't, either. Sure, he told me not to blame myself, but that hardly said anything about how he felt.

I couldn't face him, I could only look to the forest floor below, watching each and every step I took, watching each step Merlin took. I had to be vigilant, I had to make sure. To make up for injuring him.

As I grappled with my own internal turmoil, the world around me slipped into an indistinct fog.

~~~

How long has it been? Seconds? Minutes? Hours? I couldn't remember. Everything was a blur. Where are we even? How far have we traveled? When will dusk set in?

Wrapped up in my thoughts as I was, I didn't notice the tapping at my shoulder, even as it grew from light taps to gentle nudges.

Merlin grabbed my shoulder, tight, and not because of the terrain. I was watching. "Lala!" he shouted, shaking me. "Snap out of it!"

I flinched and the trance was broken. I stopped dead in my tracks and my eyes trailed upward to meet his.

"Sorry. What's wrong?" I asked numbly.

"I was asking if you were hungry. I'm guessing you didn't hear that or the hour of one-sided conversation before that." He replied, eyes full of concern and worry.

My eyes widened as I said, *"Hour?"*

He nodded with a frown.

I shook my head before letting it fall into my hand as I said, "I'm sorry, I didn't mean to worry you."

He suddenly pulled me into a light embrace before he said, "It's not your fault. I got injured because of the game I started. We will make it there on time. Please, stop worrying."

I wrapped my arms around him too and nodded.

Suddenly the snap of a twig made us both jump and spin around in a defensive position. Merlin yelps in pain due to his injured ankle and I threw my arm over to help him stay on his feet. Voices, then loud footsteps on dry leaves.

I put a finger to my lips, signaling to Merlin, who was still drawn back in pain.

The footsteps grew louder, and all at once, a resounding shout pierced the air.

They found us.

"Grab them! Don't let them get away!" yelled a seemingly human man as he motioned for his group to surround us.

We couldn't run with Merlin's injury. We were trapped. There was no way out.

"What do you want with us!"

"Zip it, sugarplum. You answer to us, not the other way around." The man said with a snarl.

"Leave her alone!" Merlin yelled, defensive.

"Look it here, men. We have ourselves a lover boy." The human cackled, his laughter resonating through the air, and his soldiers joined in with echoing jeers. The cacophony of their taunts and laughter created a discordant symphony that reverberated in the atmosphere. Merlin's face turned beet red as he grit his teeth.

"Merlin," I muttered to him, "just leave it alone. It isn't worth it."

"Y'know, you should listen to the pretty little elf girl. I guess she's the one with the brains." Another human male, seemingly much younger than the first, said, strangely half-heartedly. Almost like he didn't want to be there.

"Gordon, do not speak unless spoken to." The first man said almost in a low growl.

The boy lowered his head and clenched his fist before nodding.

"Why do you choose violence?" Maybe if he had doubts, maybe, maybe I could kindle that to help us out of our predicament.

"Excuse me? I couldn't quite hear you. Do you mind speaking up?" The human leader spat at me, his expression furious as his words.

I didn't repeat myself. Nothing for this man. I looked away from him, disgusted.

"You…" His hand reared back.

It happened in a moment. I didn't see it happen, but from the sting of my cheek and my body hitting the ground, hard, what had happened was unmistakable. All I could do was sit there in the dirt, stunned, with my hand on my beet-red cheek and tears involuntary cascading down my face.

"Don't you ever… lay a finger on her again." Merlin huffed with a new kind of wrath I've never ascertained.

"Or else what, lover boy." The man said, rolling his eyes, clearly not taking either of us seriously.

"Or, I'll *kill* you." It was scary to hear the way he said it, and I could swear I could hear his teeth grit when he spoke, could feel electricity in the air, like lightning about to strike.

The man erupted into laughter at Merlin's response. "You? Kill me? Hah! This kid is hilarious." He continued cackling, encouraging the laughter of his soldiers. The mere idea was just a joke to him. We were smaller than him, barely worth a thought, never mind caution.

Merlin began to take a step forward, but I grabbed the hem of his long coat. "Merlin, please don't. Don't do this. Please."

He looked at my bruising red cheek and then into my pleading, tear-filled eyes. His head dropped and his clenched fist relaxed. He sighed. "Fine."

"That's what I thought," said the man with a huff and a look of superiority. "Round them up, men. Looks like we have some new *guests*."

My first thought was that they were treating us like cattle, tying us with thick, coarse rope.

I wish that were the case. You don't kick cattle, don't beat it as it's laid helpless on the ground.

I looked toward the hesitant one, Gordon. He winces, but looks away from me. He presses his heavy boot into Merlin's side halfheartedly.

"No!" I wailed "Stop! You'll kill him!"

"Relax, sugarplum. We ain't going to kill him," said the hostile leader. Then, a creepy grin crept across his face. "Not yet, anyway."

My heart plummeted from my chest.

This is my fault.

As the cruel men gagged and blindfolded us, I reached out to whatever I could. My magic was unresponsive, I couldn't use it while bound. I begged prayer to the Great Willow Tree, for aid, for mercy, for protection, if not for me, then for Merlin, who I got into this mess.

I apologized for everything I could think of, for leaving, for being inadequate, for pranking my brother on his first morning home, for lying to my sister, for failing, for being ungrateful for what I had. For ever having wanted to leave.

It was all for naught. No help came, and we were carried away, abducted by some foul group of miscreants.

CHAPTER 5

Acta non verba. "Deeds, not words". While words hold their own significance, it is through our deeds that we truly shape the world around us. Deeds transcend mere rhetoric and transform intentions into tangible impact. They become the structure of trust, the currency of authenticity, and the foundation of lasting connections. In a world drowning with empty words and unfulfilled promises, it's actions that stand as a testament to our commitment, our integrity, and our ability to effect positive change. In this regard, my name is one of the most important things to me. Ilana is the name I was given by my father. It means "tree" in honor of the blessing given to me by our Great Willow Tree itself, as a small strand of seeds from the tree's branches was bestowed upon my infant chest.

How far I have fallen just for a taste of adventure. Had it been fate that led me astray or my own ignorance? And what of my name now? The rhythmic sound of horse hooves hitting the ground and the pull of the ropes that bound us tore nightmarish pain into me. Regardless of the grunts of agony that escaped my lungs, the pain continued. It felt as though we were tugged along for hours, stumbling blindly over every root we once walked carefully to avoid, some destination unknown. What would become of our lives when we reached that destination?

Worst of all, not a word or mumble had come from Merlin, nor had the sound of his light footsteps been recognizable. I had no way of knowing what had become of him since the beginning of this. Clop, clop, clop. Grunt, grunt, grunt. Huff, huff, huff. My mind raced. If I perish within the next few days, would my name have been given to me for nothing? Was its importance defiled by my own actions? Would I fail to live up to the expectations my parents envisioned for me? *Why?*

The sudden forward thrust of my body alerted me that we had arrived at the location these men had intended. The atmosphere was thick with tension, and the air felt charged with an eerie anticipation. As I tried to steady myself, the gravity of the situation sank in, and I braced for whatever awaited us in this ominous place. My knees, now scraped and burned from the impact of the ground, stung like a swarm of hornets.

"Take them to the holding cells," said a familiar unsettling voice. "And make sure you separate them. I don't want them trying anything."

Them? So that means that Merlin is still here. He's alive, but for how long? My thoughts grew even more obscured as I perceived the shift in terrain and the distinct sound of stone beneath my dirt-covered and mangled feet. The slam of a weighty door closing echoed through the air as we marched into an unfamiliar building and descended a spiral staircase. As we descended, the air grew colder and a damp chill settled in. With each step further from the world and deeper into the yawning abyss neither of us could see, foreboding draped itself tighter and tighter around us. I clung to whatever meager shreds of courage I could muster, my heart pounding in time with the echoing footsteps that reverberated through the narrow, stone-walled passage. Without my sight, my other senses seemed to become heightened, the feeling of the rough cloth over my eyes more distinct and every sound became louder and clearer. A screeching squeak from a heavy door's unoiled hinges pierced my sensitive ears just moments before a rough hand forced me to my knees. I felt the cold metal of a blade wedge between my hands and the rope that constrained them, followed by the immediate release of pressure from around my tender wrists. This was quickly followed by the sudden return of my vision which caused me to blink rapidly as the blindfold was removed.

"Make any sudden moves and I'll have to cut up that pretty face of yours," He pressed his cold, crisp dagger against my cheek, then gently dragged it down my neck, stopping at my collarbone. His eyes following the movement, he chuckled. "And we wouldn't want that, would we, beautiful?"

I shivered. I didn't want to give him the satisfaction he clearly got, with a cruel smile taking over his face, but I couldn't help it. I was cold, I was scared, I was alone. I couldn't be brave in that moment, not when innumerable horrible fates flashed through my mind.

Most of all, I feared for what had happened to Merlin. The weight of our separation pressed heavily on me. The bond we had forged through our shared experiences felt like a lifeline, and the prospect of facing the unknown without his presence sent a chill down my spine. He was just as alone as I, and I had no doubt he was just as scared, though perhaps he was more brave about it.

He might not even blame me. That thought sat heavy in my stomach, even as I dropped to the ground, curling my knees tight against my chest to fight against the encroaching chill.

Time blurred. In that deep, dark cell, I had no way to tell day from night. Minutes could be hours, could be days and weeks, for all the depths would share. My cobblestone cell was cold and confined so much that I couldn't properly lie down. My only light came from the tiny rectangular slit in the large metal door that sealed me inside that nightmare. I felt weak from the tiny tasteless scraps of bread I had been given as a substitute for food and the miniscule amount of liquid pretending to pass as water. It was enough to drive even the most grounded person insane. In this personalized penitentiary, the weight of isolation settled like a shroud, enveloping every inch of my being in an unrelenting embrace. The starkness of the walls, illuminated only by a faint shred of dim light, felt like a relentless reminder of my solitude. The air hung heavy with a palpable silence, broken only by the distant echoes of my own breath. The walls closed in, crushing like my loneliness. As the chill seeped into my bones, it carried with it a sense of detachment from the world outside, as if I were suspended in a void where time held no meaning. The only thing that pulled me out of the lake of ink that I was drowning in was the slight hope that Merlin was still alive. The sound of footsteps coming in my direction snapped my mind out of its despair-filled slumber. The sound of the lock turning, releasing the door's seal filled me with fear as the hope I had felt was diminishing.

"Get up and turn to face the back wall," said a gruff voice I didn't recognize.

I obeyed his commands. I had no other option. I felt a gritty, old rope wrap tightly around my wrists, cuffing them behind my back to prevent me from attempting to escape. Without a word, I was pushed out of the cell and down a long corridor. The light dripping of water was the only other sound in this dungeon aside from shuffled footsteps belonging to me and my captor. I felt less afraid. I felt… less. Numbed from my isolation or distracted by the dull pangs of hunger, I couldn't be certain. I could feel the darkness cloud the emotionless tinted windows that lay sunken in my skull. In the depths of my being, an unsettling stillness prevailed, as if the wellspring of emotions had completely run dry. The world outside the walls that confined me carried on with its vibrant colors and intricate melodies, but I was no longer part of them. It was as if I were observing life through a distant lens, the hues of feelings muted to grayscale.

We came to a halt in front of a cobblestone staircase, only to start again, climbing it and exit through another large metal door. All it led to was another long corridor, but this time it was well lit. My eyes watered at the sudden vibrant light, struggling to adjust after who knew how long in the dark.

Then, more walking, even as I blinked away spots dancing in my vision and stumbled over my feet. I grew tired. I hadn't moved more than a couple of inches for the duration of my imprisonment. And why was I now? I didn't care, why should I walk, carry myself to whatever doom they held in store for me?

Before I thought to stop, I was pushed to the ground. My knees, still aching from the scrapes and bruises on them, hit a cold floor. I was conscious... probably. I could hear and see things around me, but I *felt* nothing, vacant as unconsciousness.

"Here she is. I don't know how much talking she'll be doing though," spoke the gruff voice of my escort.

"That's fine. I just need to use her to get *him* to talk." In the haze of my mind, I remembered that voice. *'Relax, sugarplum.'*

Before looking up, questions about who *he* was circled in my mind. A sliver of hope pierced that barrier of misery and I felt my eyes light up for the first time in a long while. Beside him stood Merlin who had his back turned. His long coat and messenger bag were missing, but I still knew it was him.

"Look who's here, lover boy." He spun Merlin around to face me, and, even numb as I was, I still felt the horror that clawed at me when I saw his face. Blacked and bruised, scraped and bleeding sluggishly. His eyes widened the moment they met mine.

"Lala! You're-" Merlin started, but was cut off by an angry voice.

"You speak when you are spoken to, prisoner."

"Boris, if I may." A thin hand appeared on the man I had taken to be the leader's shoulder. "Perhaps allowing me to hold onto the girl during this... interrogation would be a wise decision, yes? Thus allowing us to have this broad specimen to guard the door, hm?"

"Yes, you are right." Boris jerked his head, motioning to the guard to get into position.

"Greetings, insignificant creatures!" The third man, the one with wit and without bulk, strode forward, spreading his arms as if basking in a nonexistent spotlight. "I am Alastor. Don't forget it, now. I will be taking things from here." He slunk behind me, then wrapped an arm around my arm. I whimpered as he yanked me to my feet, and at the tight grip he moved to my shoulder. ."

"Now," Alastor said, his voice reveling in the anger Merlin couldn't seem to hide. "Let's get started shall we?"

With that, he promptly swiped a dagger from behind his back and held it tightly against my throat, pressing into my skin without breaking it. Not yet, anyway.

"No! Don't touch her!" Merlin screamed, but he paid for that with a doubtlessly painful kick in the abdomen from Boris.

"I won't need to hurt her, so long as you answer my questions honestly." I had no way to see his face, but I could hear the slimy smile in his stupid voice.

Merlin's face went from enraged to defeated. I could tell that he felt trapped and helpless, knowing that my life was on the line. In that moment, his defeat mirrored my own, a shared recognition of the dire straits we found ourselves in. The unspoken connection between us remained steadfast, even as the grip of uncertainty tightened around us, reminding us that our destinies were inextricably linked, for better or for worse.

"Question number one. Who are you, and who is she?"

"I am Merlin. Human. She is Lala, a stray elf." Merlin answered as blandly as possible to avoid giving away too much information.

Alastor appeared to pick up on this though as he grasped me tighter, ignoring my hiss of pain. "Tsk tsk, naughty, naughty. You're going to have to answer better than that." He tapped his blade against my skin. Any time he could have chosen to cut me, rather than tease Merlin with threats.

"Stop! Okay, fine. I will give you more information, just don't hurt her." Merlin pleaded.

"Who. Are. You?"

"I am Merlin Grimold of Camelot. What I told you about Lala is all I know." Alastor pressed the knife against my skin. "It's all I know, I swear! I swear!"

"The prince, hm? We've hit the jackpot, boys!"

"Leave him alone." I hissed.

Alastor dug his fingers into my shoulder. "You'll keep that pretty mouth of yours shut if you know what's good for you," he hissed into my ear.

I winced in pain again, unable to keep it from my face.

"Next question!" The pressure eased but didn't disappear. "And I do so hope you aren't lying to us. Where were you imbeciles headed?" Alaster asked, causing Boris to snicker.

"What does it matter to you?" Merlin retorted.

"Ah ah ah. Wrong answer!" With the grip he had on my shoulder, it was easy for Alastor to spin me to face him.

I felt terror return to my mind as Alastor glared deep into my eyes. All I could see was a chilling, empty darkness belonging only to a madman. The intensity of his stare sent shivers down my spine, a threat that loomed large, a harbinger of some unknown evil, a vast and looming threat I could not understand. At first, all I perceived was a flash of light, catching off some metal object. Then reality caught up with me, and I realized it was the knife, cutting through my skin, darkening my ruined clothes with blood.

My blood. I felt gravity seize my body, pulling it to the ground. I heard a bone-chilling shrill escape from Merlin's throat, the sound slicing through the air like the blade had me. The sheer anguish that resonated in that sound was impossible to ignore, a gut-wrenching manifestation of the torment he was enduring.

I could barely hear it, barely see the horrified dismay on his face. Everything felt even more distant than it had before like I was looking out through a deep fog.

"Now where was I? Ah, yes. Where are you headed?"

"C-Camelot," stuttered Merlin.

"Very good! See? It isn't that hard," said Alastor, contemptuously.

The room around me was blurring and fading. I couldn't move. I couldn't speak. I wanted to assure Merlin, tell him I was okay, tell him not to worry about me.

"Now. Why were you insignificant little weaklings headed to Camelot? Going home to cry to your mommy?"

Merlin looked away, not knowing how to answer.

With a sigh, Alastor said, "Shame, shame. It's really not this difficult to answer a question. Oh well, the only one to blame for this is you."

With that he leaned over, plunging his blade into my side. The searing pain caused me to scream.

"No! Lala!" Merlin wailed as his voice became shaky.

"Hmm, let's give her a few little beauty marks shall we?" Alastor inquired sarcastically as he rapidly slashed my forehead once and my cheek twice. He hummed, tilting his head to examine the damage he had done as if it were brush strokes and not knife slashes. He tilted his head to Merlin. "Now, what do we think?"

"Leave her alone!" Merlin screamed, lunging at Alastor only to be restrained by Boris.

"Now that is a no-no," said Alastor firmly, standing and walking over to Merlin. He leaned over him. "Never." He tapped the bloody knife against Merlin's face, leaving a thin streak of blood in its wake. "And I do mean *never*, attempt to attack me again."

Merlin's head dropped in defeat. I felt the pool under my body grow as my blood continued to spill from my wounds. In the shadow of the unknown, the cold hand of death seemed to inch closer with every passing heartbeat. The air grew heavy with a sense of inevitability as if time itself were conspiring to bring me face to face with the great abyss. The world seemed to dim, its colors muted by the looming specter of mortality. With each breath, I felt the weight of existence pressing down, the awareness that the boundary between life and death was tenuous and ephemeral.

"And I certainly can't let something like that go unpunished now, can I?" He returned to his place and crouched over me. "Where should we add... ah, why complicate things?" I was too numb to track where he stabbed, again and again and again. Too tired to count, again and again and again.

For the first time since this had all begun, Merlin couldn't contain his emotions as they broke through his fractured barrier and a flood of tears streamed out of his eyes. His sobs snapped Alastor out of his bloodthirsty craze and he returned to a standing upright position. His clothes and his face were drenched in my elvish mulberry blood. Merlin collapsed to the ground, resting on his knees as he wept. All of the stress and anguish escaped from him at once as if his bottle of emotions finally shattered. As I flickered before him, a slight pang of sorrow pierced through the shell of numbness that had enveloped me. His vulnerability, once hidden behind a facade of strength, lay exposed like shards of glass catching the light. The hazy sight of his emotions breaking free was like a fragile melody resonating within the silence. At that moment, the icy grip of my own detachment thawed, allowing a fleeting echo of empathy to seep in. The sight of Merlin's despair laid bare tore me back. I wanted to rush over to comfort him, but my battered body forbade it.

Ah." The grin was audible in his voice. "That's where we wanted to be." He patted my cheek, smearing my own blood on my face. "Good girl. Boris!"

Alastor handed his dagger over to Boris' waiting hands and held his own out over me, consumed by a strange crimson light. My body felt tingly as strange magical energy was transferred into it, partially healing my wounds. I watched weakly as my wounds began to close before my eyes. Although my physical wounds began to heal, my emotional state remained unchanged. Pain and fear continued to gnaw at the edges of my thoughts, unwilling to be so easily forgotten. Once it was deemed that my wounds were no longer fatal, Alastor dropped his hands and turned to Boris.

"Summon Gordon, I need my blade cleansed."

In my hazy mind, I only half recognized the name. Gordon. The hesitant one.

"Alastor, he's only a kid. Is this really a-" Boris started, but was cut off by Alastor's cold expression.

"Do as you are told, Boris. That kid needs to grow a backbone or he's useless."

Boris frowned and closed his eyes. A strange crest on his forearm I hadn't noticed earlier started to glow a deep garnet. Soon enough, there was a gentle knock at the door.

"You may enter, Gordon," Alastor spoke out.

The door handle turned and a green-haired boy entered whom I hadn't recognized since he wasn't wearing his armor. Gordon's expression went from curious to aghast as he examined the bloody, gut-wrenching scene that lay before him. His remorseful eyes gazed down at me and then darted over to Merlin who was still bawling. The sight of Gordon's expression as his eyes fell upon the harrowing tableau of blood splatters and heartbroken sobs, his features contorting with a mixture of dismay and disgust, would forever haunt me. Gordon's once composed demeanor faltered, his countenance betraying the shock he felt. The cacophony of despair and the macabre imagery painted a vivid picture of tragedy, and the turmoil etched across his face mirrored the turmoil within his soul.

"Gordon, go clean this disgusting dagger for me will you?" Alastor said, bored and uncaring for the emotional damage he was causing.

Gordon didn't react, as if he was paralyzed in fear. The innocence that radiated from his gaze was a poignant reminder of the stark divide between his life and ours, a divide that had been further widened by our captivity. At that moment, I couldn't help but feel a pang of bittersweet envy for his ignorance, a longing for the days when I too could view the world with such unguarded innocence.

"Hello? Earth to Gordon," said Alastor.

Still no response. Gordon hastily spun around only to lean over and regurgitate what was once his lunch all over the filthy blood-drenched floor.

"Sheesh, man up, kid," Alastor said as he shook his head. "Clean this up when you are done with your little introspection over there."

"W-why? Why would you do this, sir Alastor?" Gordon murmured in disbelief.

"Don't speak unless spoken to!" Boris demanded before Alastor raised his hand to stop him.

He sighed. "Because, kid. This world is either kill or be killed. I want the power to have that choice. You'll understand when you stop being so damn naive." Alastor's voice dipped into a vicious growl.

Gordon shook his head, still processing what he had witnessed as he spoke softly with a disgusted tone, "I would understand protecting yourself, but this… this isn't right."

"Now now, Gordon. You wouldn't dare defy me now, would you? You know the punishment for treason is death." Alastor said, provokingly.

"No, sir." Gordon frowned, knowing there was nothing he could do.

He took the blade from Boris before wistfully turning around and rushing out the door.

"Now then, take this one back to her cell," said Alastor, pointing at my mangled body before turning towards Merlin. "And I will take care of him."

Still too injured to speak, I gazed at Merlin. I felt dismay consume my once emotionless mind as I felt Boris throw my body over his shoulder and carry me back to my hellish confinement.

The atmosphere felt stagnant. I couldn't bring myself to eat or drink, my body stung from the injuries I had sustained, but all the while I only truly worried for Merlin's well-being. Not only that, I now worried for Gordon, who had his innocence stripped from him. I hated feeling hopeless. I hated that I was weak. I hated all of it. I continued to lay in this pit of despair, wondering if there would ever be a way out. Alas, all hope was lost along with my compassion. That was until I heard a faint, inaudible whisper. I forced my body upright through the arduous pain in an attempt to fully awaken myself in fear that I was hallucinating.

"Pssst. Hey, are you down here?" whispered a familiar voice.

I tried whispering back, but my hoarse voice came out as a croak.

"Is that you? Try to make a bit more noise so that I can find you. I'm coming," said the voice.

I began repeatedly tapping my hand on the ground as it was the only part of my body that could move freely. I could hear the sound of soft footsteps coming closer and closer until they suddenly stopped. The loud click of the lock turning startled me, announcing the arrival of a mysterious savior. To my surprise, the door swung open, revealing none other than Gordon holding the key that released me from my penitentiary.

"I'm going to get you and your friend out of here," Gordon said, waving his hand over my filthy dress, suddenly cleaning it of its bloodstains and mysteriously mending the torn fabric. "I... I'll need to carry you. Are you okay with that?"

I nodded, understanding his intentions were pure. I weakly smiled at him as hope wriggled back into my soul, a fragile beacon amidst the darkness that surrounded us. In that fleeting moment, the weight of our captivity felt just a bit lighter, and the future seemed less bleak. He carefully lifted my body off of the ground and began walking opposite to where I had already been.

"It'll be okay," Gordon assured me, "I know where they're keeping him."

My eyes stung with tears that I was too dehydrated to cry, and my cheeks ached from the smile that I couldn't help but offer him.

I could trust Gordon. It would be okay.

"I also set up mana-controlled detonators around this facility over the past few hours. I'm not a violent person, but... but I don't end this now, more people will die because of them."

I tried to speak, but all I managed was a weak croak. He glanced down at me, though, so I nodded at him, trying to assure him.

He smiled, and the warmth of his smile was a balm to my wounded spirit.

"Once we get out of here, I will fully heal your wounds. It's just too risky to do that now. I'm sorry."

I nodded, then let my head loll to the side so I could look at our surroundings. We started traveling up a long spiral staircase before stopping at another heavy metal door. Gordon fumbled with balancing my limp body and operating the handle. Eventually, he managed.

"He should be down this corridor. After we retrieve him we will head to the door at the top of that staircase, then turn right. The exit is straight ahead." Gordon said informatively.

As the corridor ahead shortened, I teetered on the sharp edge of uncertainty. How badly would he be injured? My heart was pounding out of my chest. The fear of Merlin's dire condition gripped me like a vice, the shadows of potential loss casting a pall over my thoughts. The gravity of the situation loomed large, casting its dark shadow over my feeble hope.

"Here, he should be in here," said Gordon. He pulled a new key out of his pocket and inserted it into the door's lock.

With a twist, Gordon quietly opened the door and I felt my heart soar through my chest as I saw Merlin lying on the ground, asleep with seemingly few injuries.

"Don't scream," Gordon said as he gently tapped Merlin with his foot.

Merlin jumped to his feet, startled by the sudden disruption to his slumber.

"What are you-" Merlin started before his gaze shifted to me, "Lala!"

"Shhh! You have to be quiet, or they'll hear us. Hurry, we don't have much time." Gordon urged Merlin to follow us out of the corridor and back to the spiral staircase.

The staircase felt eternal, each step drawing us sluggishly closer to freedom. After what felt like dozens of lifetimes, we reached the top of the staircase and exited out the door. Gordon was right. He opened the heavy wooden door in front of us with his free hand, and a light, refreshing breeze wrapped around our bodies and the crisp evening moonlight illuminated our path to freedom.

"We only have until dawn. Run!" Gordon sprinted toward the treeline. He gently laid me down behind a tree before patting the ground as if he was looking for something.

"What are you doing?" Merlin asked confusedly.

"I used invisibility magic to hide our belongings. I just need to find them," Gordon said, not looking at Merlin as he worked. Then, triumphantly, he declared, "Here they are!"

With the snap of his fingers, a leaf green spark jolted from his fingertips and a pile of items appeared out of nowhere beside the tree. Among the items were Merlin's long coat, spell book, and messenger bag along with an unfamiliar bow and quiver of silver arrows.

"I thought you would want it back."

"How didn't you get caught?" Merlin asked, astonished at Gordon's stealth.

"No one really pays attention to me," Gordon said, smiling wryly. Then he turned to the structure we had just escaped from.

"You may want to cover your ears for this next part."

Once we had, he stepped out from our cover, his feet aligned and shoulders squared. He threw his arms out to his side to form a star with his body. A green light outlined him before glowing brighter around his hands, illuminating the night sky. Keeping his arms straight, he slammed his hands together in front of him, and a strange bow, made of the same green light as the aura around him appeared in his hands. As he drew the string back, an arrow appeared. I could feel the energy of the land and even the energy within myself flowing into him. It was awe-inspiring, but confounding. How could that be possible? Only the elvish race knows druid magic, so how does this human know how to channel it? I watched, perplexed and amazed as he drew his arm back to release the arrow of green light which scattered mid-air before landing in several different areas around the building. Explosions followed instantly, further coloring the magical light show that purged the night sky of its darkness. I was utterly speechless, maintaining a locked gaze on the evanescent display as the darkness returned to claim its territory, snuffing out the light. All that was left was pure silence. No talking. No critters chirping their midnight tune. Nothing.

"Wow. That was… something you don't see every day." Merlin said in an attempt to break the silence.

Gordon collapsed to his knees, panting for breath, but laughing nonetheless.

"Are you alright?" Merlin asked as he sat down beside both of us.

"I'll be fine. I just… used too much energy. We need to get a fair distance away from here," he said, struggling to get back on his feet. "I'm sure other beings heard that explosion and it may not be safe to remain here for very long."

"I'll carry Lala. Do you need any help?"

"Nah lad, I can manage." He leaned against a tree, but he was standing, which was more than I could do.

Merlin nodded as He tenderly raised my body from its earthy resting place. I glanced over at Gordon, who was struggling to walk. Quickly and instinctively, I twirled my finger to create a sturdy walking aid made of dense vines with an added hint of wood.

"Don't use your magic right now. You're far too weak and your body doesn't have the energy to spare," said Gordon before sighing, noticing my disappointment in his response. "Still. Thank you."

Then, we set off. The moonlight struggled to reach us through the foliage, but we kept going. We may have met on different sides, but with the destruction we fled, there was no question that now, in this quiet night, we had become comrades.

The forest breathed with life around us, but we were alone.

"It feels so good to be outside again," I said, looking up at Merlin who was staring straight forward.

"Yeah… I'm not sure how long it's been since we've gotten to feel the crisp fresh air refresh our bodies." Merlin replied, though his expression didn't change.

"Oh, I can answer that," Gordon says. "It's been two weeks since you were taken by Boris."

"Two weeks?!" Merlin and I said loudly in unison.

"Yep. Two whole weeks of solitude. I couldn't imagine being in your position." Gordon looked down at his feet, suffocating from the sorrow and guilt he felt.

"Hey, you got us out of there. That's what matters."

He half smiled at me, acknowledging my efforts to cheer him up. His expression held a hint of gratitude, a silent recognition of the small yet meaningful gestures that connected us in moments of hardship.

"Gordon, I really hope you can help me gather my bearings and set us on the right track toward our destination," Merlin said with a concerned look on his face.

"Don't fret, I know these woods like the back of my hand. I often hunt out here."

"Ah, so you're a hunter? That explains the bow and arrows."

"Yep! I've known how to shoot ever since I could carry a bow!" Gordon chuckled.

"Your bow," I remember. "It's lovely."

"Ah, thank you, lass," Gordon nodded to me. His voice was fond as he explained, "I made this one myself. Crafted from the finest wood and coated with a beautiful silver finish."

"Gordon, I've been meaning to ask you something for a little while now-" I started but then paused, questioning whether or not my curiosity would be considered prying.

"Yes? What is it, love?" His curious pine-green eyes shimmered as he spoke.

"How did you learn to use druid magic? I thought only elves could use it?" I asked.

"Whoever said I was human?" Gordon grinned as he waved his hand around his head, revealing short elvish ears from behind his illusion magic.

"Your ears… you are elvish!" I said in astonishment.

"Half elvish," he chimed in, "My mother was an elf belonging to the eastern woodland elvish colony and my father was a human from Camelot. I am but a half-breed."

I was surprised and judging by Merlin's expression I could tell that he was as well.

"Wait, you're from Camelot?" Merlin asked, baffled by Gordon's words.

"I didn't say that," he stated, "I've never been to Camelot myself, but I heard it's a beautiful place."

"Wait, then where did you grow up as a kin?" I asked curiously.

"I grew up where my mother did, in the eastern elvish colony." Gordon smiled, "My father thought it safer to grow up there instead of among the humans."

I nodded, empathizing with him before looking up at Merlin only to see confusion in his eyes. How was he supposed to know? He himself was a human.

"Elves are targeted for a plethora of reasons by other races. The reasons are... quite harsh and selfish." I frowned as I spoke, knowing that elves were seen as weak and pure which made them vulnerable.

"For years, the elvish colonies had been targeted because of their druid properties. Our sisters and brothers had been murdered, kidnapped, and even sold as slaves to cruel buyers from other races." Gordon said, finishing the idea I had started.

"Oh my! I never knew that. I'm so sorry," Merlin said, bewildered by the barbarism of other beings.

"This is why so many races have gone without seeing us. We are safe within our hidden colonies, but without them, we are at fate's mercy," I said.

"That makes sense then why I haven't seen an elf before you, Lala," Merlin realized.

I nodded, unable to say more. The burden of our ancestors' experiences and the implicit recognition of the cruelty our elvish race had endured were sufficient to fill the silence that lingered in the atmosphere.

"On a brighter note, I believe we could start making camp here," Gordon said as he slowly came to a stop.

I started to raise my hand to create a campsite like I had before, but Gordon gently grasped my hand and shook his head.

"Lala, we will take care of it this time. Don't overdo it, especially not when you are in this condition." Merlin said, worriedly.

"Our bodies can only withstand so much, lass. Take it easy and relax." Gordon added.

I nodded sadly as Merlin gently laid me on the soft grass and patted my head lightly.

"I appreciate your attempt to conate, but I ask that you close your eyes and rest," Gordon said before walking off to grab stones to create an outline for the campfire.

"I promise, you will be alright. Please sleep," Merlin said before he too walked off to gather resources for our bivouac.

In the blink of an eye, I was alone again, but not truly *alone*. It didn't hurt as it had before. Instead, I felt a warm fuzzy feeling deep within my chest. This feeling felt new because of the emptiness I had felt not even a day earlier. We finally did it. We finally escaped from there. It was this feeling that swept me into the night's charm, lulling me to sleep.

CHAPTER 6

Abundans cautela non nocet, or "one can never be too careful", was something my father would always say to me when I was a child. I was quite bashful in my youth; curious, brave, even a little reckless. Nothing seems to have changed really. I was still foolish enough to make the same mistakes over and over, hoping for a rescuer. All I had ever wanted was the strength to choose my own fate, to fight against all odds and emerge victorious. When times were tough and Merlin needed me, I still wasn't strong enough. The weight of my own limitations bore down on me, a stark reminder that even the most fervent desires could be tempered by the harsh reality of one's own vulnerabilities. In those moments of weakness, I couldn't help but feel a pang of frustration, a yearning to possess the unwavering strength I had always longed for. This reality haunted my slumber to its core before the sudden shaking of my shoulder transported me from my inner labyrinth back to my existence.

"Lala! Wake up, wake up, wake up." Merlin said excitedly.

As the morning haze clouded my mind, I cast a curious gaze at him while I gradually sat up.

"Camelot!" Merlin almost squealed, overwhelmed with joy. "We're right outside of Camelot!"

"We must have traveled further than I originally thought, lass. We've made it to your destination." Gordon smiled at Merlin's enthusiasm.

In awe, my gaze was fixed beyond the tree line as I beheld a colossal kingdom enclosed by a formidable protective wall. The walls, constructed from imposing stone and adorned with intricate carvings, rose high into the sky, a testament to the grandeur that lay within. Towers stretched toward the heavens, their spires touching the clouds, flags of vibrant colors fluttered in the breeze, proudly displaying the kingdom's sigils. The sight was both majestic and humbling, proudly announcing the history and power that resided within those walls. As I took in the sight, a mixture of excitement and trepidation coursed through me, knowing that our journey was about to intersect with the heart of this sprawling realm. The cover of darkness the previous night must have caused us to miss it. Things seemed to be looking up for us. After weeks, almost months of travel, we had finally arrived.

"Well what are we waiting for? Let's go!" I hurriedly attempted to get to my feet only to be halted by searing pain all over my body as I had forgotten my injuries in the heat of the moment.

"Easy does it, lass. I still need to heal you. I didn't have the energy last night after setting off the detonations." Gordon said as he held his hands over me as I returned to a seated upright position.

His hands were engulfed by a bright green light for only a few moments and I felt my pain slowly melt away. The once-deep gashes vanished from my pale soft skin and a feeling of refreshment fell over me. I felt great and more energetic than I ever had before!

"How do you feel?" Merlin asked, his eyes shimmering with hope.

"Good as new!" I said cheerfully.

"Alrighty then, let's go to Camelot!" Gordon said eagerly.

We quickly packed up the small amount of gear we had and made our way towards the mighty stone brick wall that guarded the perimeter of Camelot. I was both optimistic and anxious to see the land of Merlin's people, and my heart fluttered with a mix of anticipation and uncertainty. The landscape that stretched before us was unfamiliar, yet the presence of Merlin by my side offered a sense of familiarity and connection that grounded me. As we stepped forward into this new realm, I couldn't help but wonder what challenges and discoveries awaited us within its borders. I was eager to learn the mannerisms of the humanfolk and converse with them, to gain insights into their culture and ways of life. The prospect of engaging with a new community and broadening my understanding of the world beyond my own was exhilarating. Each step forward was a chance to bridge the gap between our worlds and forge connections that transcended differences. I never thought a life of longing for adventure would have led me to this moment. I felt overwhelmed with joy, both for Merlin and myself. Seeing Merlin's homeland, his roots, and the potential for him to reconnect with his people was a source of happiness well-needed for the both of us.

Excitement swelled within me as the walls grew taller. There was so much I could learn, within those gates, so many opportunities for us both. Merlin could go home, and I finally would get to meet his royal family! I would be the first royal elf to have met the king and queen of a human civilization!

From the heights of excitement, I fell hard, suddenly remembering the web of lies I had spun. The weight of the deception I had carried gnawed at my conscience. While I yearned to embrace the new experiences ahead, the heavy guilt of my falsehoods and the weighty consequences they promised pulled my heart to my stomach.

Worries circled in my mind, swooping like vultures. How could I tell Merlin that I had been lying to him the whole time? Would he believe me, now, so far from anyone who could vouch for me? Would he *forgive* me? Could he? Should he, even, forgive someone who had joined him under false pretenses? I felt lost, unaware of what to do. I could tell him the truth and risk our friendship or keep it to myself and risk him finding out the truth. Dirty lies plagued me and only now had I noticed how far I had fallen. I had to tell him the truth.

I just needed to wait for the right time.

It wasn't important yet, I rationalized to myself. It was a little white lie, and the truth could wait until his sister was healed, no matter how heavily my sin weighed on my shoulders.

A sudden halt startled me and I tripped over my own feet, bumping into Merlin before grinning sheepishly at my lack of attention.

"I almost forgot. We are not accustomed to seeing elves, especially not in our own territory. It might be best if you hide your ears." He seemed apologetic, at least.

"Already ahead of you, Merlin." Gordon proclaimed with a twirl of his finger, and in an instant, both his ears and mine vanished from sight.

It felt strange, and I couldn't help but laugh. "I'm seriously never going to get used to that."

The boys joined in, and we all shared a laugh before proceeding to the open front gate of Camelot, our spirits lightened.

The town was very lively, full of busy villagers trading goods and going about their daily lives. I was captivated by the humans. Their daily routines were so different compared to what I had known, I wanted to learn and see more. I wanted to understand the young women in oddly colored dresses who were working, rushing in and out of buildings with food and goods. I wanted to understand the young men running around buying and selling products. Above all, I wanted to understand the playful children who were roaming around the streets playing unfamiliar games of hopping between chalk-drawn squares and jumping rope.

Merlin gently tugged me out of my awed, fascinated daze and back into motion. He almost seemed concerned that I would unintentionally draw too much attention to myself, and I couldn't blame him. I was acting very out of place, though thankfully no one seemed to notice or care. Gordon also seemed to be intrigued with this new environment in which we had immersed ourselves.

"You two need to act more natural. You can observe later, but first I need to get to my sister." Merlin said, slightly annoyed with our behavior.

Gordon and I both nodded sheepishly.

Turning a corner, our eyes widened at the sight before us: a massive drawbridge, a grand gateway to the royal castle, guarded by no fewer than four knights. The scene unfolded like a tale from a storybook, the imposing drawbridge the threshold to the heart of Camelot's power and authority.

With a confidence he could only have from being their prince, Merlin hurried to speak with one of the guards. "Alexander. I'm back. How is my family? My sister?" Merlin asked frantically.

"How about you see for yourself? Come, come, there is no time to waste!" Alexander said before narrowing his eyes, noticing Gordon and me, "Wait. Who are these youngsters?"

"Relax, they are with me," Merlin replied, looking back at us. His voice held a gentle air of authority, and his expression read, to me, as gratitude.

Alexander fixed us with a stern gaze, his eyes narrowing before he shrugged, and then proceeded to usher us into the protective embrace of the castle walls, his demeanor a mix of authority and reluctant acquiescence.

From within the castle's interior, the sheer size of the structure loomed large, further evidence of the grandeur of Camelot's architecture. As we ventured further, the sense of awe only deepened, each corner revealing new facets of its intricate design and storied past. I found myself captivated by the exquisite spectrum of colors in the long corridors – rich reds, regal purples, vibrant greens, and even hints of tranquil blues. It was a mesmerizing journey, a visual feast of wonder. Dozens of maids and butlers scurried about, each carrying bundles of unfamiliar items. It almost reminded me of home, a bittersweet pang of nostalgia washing over me. Oh, how I missed the familiar surroundings and the comforting routines that defined my life before this journey began. In the luminous glow of the lanterns lining the hallway, a twinkle graced my eyes. The path ahead branched into a three-way fork, each route adorned with the same regal touch – an elegant carpet of red and yellow that stretched along the passages of the castle.

There was something else that stood out to me, though.

"Psst Gordon," I muttered, leaning toward him.

"Yes?" He replied softly.

"I-I'm not wearing any shoes," I murmured, feeling a tinge of embarrassment. His eyes widened, and his gaze flickered down to my feet.

"I need shoes or I'll draw attention to myself," I said, my tone tinged with worry. The prospect of standing out in such an illustrious place was enough to heighten my anxiety.

Regrettably, it was too late. The penetrating gazes of castle workers seemed to fixate on me from all directions as they passed by. Gordon's eyes widened with concern as he frantically waved his hand at my bare feet, creating the illusion of chestnut brown flats encompassing them. I scanned the hallway to see a few wide-eyed, baffled expressions and I began to sweat nervously, knowing that I had nearly blown my cover. I took a deep breath as we reached a pair of fancy walnut doors.

As the weighty doors swung open, my eyes fell upon an opulent, lavish bedroom. Within, a familial tableau unfolded: a mother, a father, a brother, and a young girl laid on the plush mattress the others surrounded, her vibrant purple hair haloed around her. Her chest rose and fell in unsteady breaths, and her skin had an ill pallor to it. Merlin hastened to join the group by the bedside of the delicate girl. He swiftly retrieved his spell book from his tawny brown bag, snapping it open as he pulled it in front of himself. Without a doubt that girl was his ill sister. Merlin's face quickly became drenched in sweat as he flipped through the pages, searching for a possible cure.

I laid my hand gently on his shoulder, hoping to reassure him. His focus remained steadfast, undeterred by my attempt to comfort him. I glanced up at his parents, their expressions marked by desperation and unease. My heart ached for them, the desperation carved into each of their faces. None of them spoke. Not to be mistaken for silence, I could hear the queen, for that is who she must be, stifling little sobs into her handkerchief.

When I looked to her, I saw the puffy, swollen redness that followed tears. "Is there anything I can do, your majesty?" I asked softly.

She couldn't answer more than a weak shake of the head, allowing a thin veil of her chocolate brown hair to shield her face for a moment. She pressed her handkerchief against her face and squeezed her eyes shut, and more tears peeked out from the edges of her eyes. The king raised a hand to his wife's face, and gently brushed the teardrops away, then laid it to rest on her shoulder. He squeezed, gently, and she leaned into him.

I clenched my teeth against my own uselessness, then shifted my focus back to Merlin, who was currently engrossed in a hushed incantation while his gaze remained fixed on an enigmatic page within his spellbook. Blinking, I tilted my head to get a better angle at the book I was only now catching a glance at the pages of. My first, confounding glance remained true. There were no words there, not even a drop of ink or even a smudged fingerprint. It was just blank. Questions circled in my mind only to be shaken away by my morality, reminding me of the predicament we found ourselves in. I refocused my attention on Merlin, who was now shrouded in a blue cloak of light. He leaned forward to gently place his magic-infused hand on his sister's torso, and she too was engulfed by Merlin's spell. I stared in awe at the expanding energy that not only flowed through Merlin into his sister but completely inundated the entire room as well. I peered over at Gordon, who had his hand on the shoulder of the man who I had assumed to be Merlin's brother. He, too, was astonished by the flow of energy that encompassed the atmosphere.

Out of nowhere, a succession of translucent lights materialized and began to sway gracefully throughout the room, casting an otherworldly glow in their wake. I could see a young boy and a young girl playing in an abundant flower garden, running around and laughing as the moving image continued. Another image captured the same boy and girl, though in this instance, the boy was carefully binding a white fabric around the young girl's knee. And above the figures of the boy and girl were portrayed once more, this time attired in proper clothing, standing before a couple who exhibited an oddly dignified demeanor. It was then that I realized what I was seeing. They weren't random lights and images. They were memories, Merlin's memories to be exact. The spectacle before me was unlike anything I had ever witnessed, an extraordinary display of energy that left me utterly astounded. I allowed my eyes to wander around the room, watching the memories of Merlin and his sister. I wasn't the only one awed. The room was enraptured.

Alas, as quickly as they appeared, the memories began to fade as Merlin's chanting did. I refocused my attention on Merlin who had removed his hand from his sister's chest and stood upright once more. Without a second to process, he collapsed to the ground beside his sister's resting place.

As I scrambled to support him, I heard a faint intake of breath escape the princess's lips. When I looked back to her, she was leaning against the headboard of her bed.

"What's going on?" She asked weakly before her eyes caught a glimpse of her parent's grief filled faces.

"Cerie?" The queen called out, falling to her knees and taking the girl's small hand into hers.

"Was I… dead?" Cerie asked guiltily.

"Shhh, it matters not, my child," the king soothed, smoothing out the hairs at her forehead and pressing a kiss to it.

They both wrapped their arms around their daughter, and, from between her parents, she laughed weakly.

Tears welled up in my eyes, and a smile spread across my face. I was relieved to see their family pieced back together, their love and unity stronger than ever. I turned my focus entirely to Merlin, limp in my arms. I pulled him to rest properly in my lap, desperate to give him something of comfort even in his unconscious state.

"He'll be okay, Lala," Gordon said affably as he placed his hand on my shoulder.

"My baby brother is a tough one. He'll be awake come morning," the man at his side assured.

"Your highness," I said, bowing my head to him as he approached, "may I ask, what is thyn name?" I respectfully inquired.

"Vulcan," he said, his shoulders tensing. "No need for all the formalities."

I blushed, my cheeks burning as I realized my lack of knowledge about proper mannerisms for human royalty had caused him discomfort.

As I worried if it had also made him suspicious of me, Vulcan chuckled, then patted my shoulder.

"You aren't from around here, are you? I recon Merlin found you along his journey for this spell to cure Cerie." He smiled as a blazing orange strand of his hair fell over his left eye.

A nervous sweat broke out on my forehead, but I reassured myself that he seemed convinced I was a human.

"Indeed he did." I hesitantly responded.

As I looked up at him, it struck me how different he looked from Merlin. Unlike Merlin, Vulcan looked strong, his muscles undeniable from hours spent training. His hair was strange, ashen gray at his roots despite the vibrant orange that danced by his face, a gradient-like flame between the two extremes.

I swallowed a lump forming in my throat as the thought that he could probably snap me in half with ease flickered, unbidden, into my mind.

"You alright, darling?" Vulcan asked, picking up on my skittish-like behavior.

"Y-yes! I'm alright!" I hastily said before pausing to recollect myself, "I'm just worried about Merlin that's all."

"Well, like I said, he is one tough cookie. He'll be fine. You'll see." Vulcan pats my shoulder once more, then picks Merlin up. "I'm sure he'll tell you himself when he wakes up."

"I sure hope so…"

In truth, it wasn't his health that worried me, but his reaction to the truth scared me to death. Would he forgive me? How could he? I had been lying to him from the start. I was dreading it. I had to tell him sooner or later. Eventually, this adventure would have to come to an end and I would have to return home. Could I return home after this? Fear once more became my worst nightmare. When I chose to accompany Merlin on his journey, I hadn't thought of the consequences my actions would have. I didn't even consider the destructive impact it would have on my loving family. How could I have done this to them? They never deserved this. The devastation of potentially losing a child is overwhelming, and I had subjected them to that anguish without a second thought Had I become a monster? I was so naive and blinded by desire that I willingly put my family through hell. How could I go back after that? How could I face my mistakes? How could I confront the demons I never realized I had?

"Hey, Lala?" Gordon leaned down, holding his hand out to me. I blushed, realizing I had been sitting on the floor despite Merlin being gone. "Let's go get some air, yeah?"

I nodded in agreement and took his hand. Back on my feet, I trailed listlessly behind Gordon as we exited the room, stepping into the vacant corridor. He walked over to the pillar in the middle of the hallway and leaned against it before gently taking my hands in his.

"What's going on with you? You seem on edge and anxious." Gordon said worriedly.

"I am just worried about Merlin, that's all," I answered sheepishly, knowing my answer was deceitful.

"Lala, you don't have to lie to me," Gordon said solemnly.

I went quiet. I felt my head drop, weighed down by the persisting conflict that continued to gnaw at my mind. I didn't know what to say or what I *should* say. I felt trapped between a rock and a hard place, with no clear path forward and the weight of my decisions pressing heavily on my back. I must have dissociated from reality once more because the gentle touch of a hand on my shoulder made me jump.

"Lala," Gordon frowned, squeezing my hands, "please. You can trust me."

I sighed and said, "It's just… I was afraid of who Merlin was and who I would run into that I got caught in a web of lies and I just-"

"Lala, an elvish princess like yourself, is always at risk in the world outside our colonies. You made the call you felt was right." Gordon said.

A sharp feeling of shock pierced my body at the realization that he saw right through my deceitful veil, leaving me exposed and vulnerable before his perceptive gaze.

"Wait, you knew? How?" I asked, dumbfoundedly.

"Your dress," he said, gesturing. "Most elves don't have fine silks like that to spare for making daily wear. Your posture is very proper too, and so is your speech."

"Is it really that obvious?" I asked, beginning to panic.

"No, not at all. It's only noticeable for those who know what to look for," Gordon tenderly reassured me.

"I just feel so trapped. I have to tell Merlin the truth eventually, but… I'm afraid." It felt good to admit it, even as my heart weighed with the knowledge that I was as bad a liar as I feared.

"You did lie, this is true, but you did it for a good reason. I'm sure if you explain it to him, he will be understanding." Gordon soothed.

"Deep down I know that, but still… I've been lying to him for several weeks now and I just-" I tumbled over my words as they caught in my chest, twisted around my breaths and the sting in my eyes.

I stumbled a bit as I found myself pulled forward into an unexpected embrace. The rush of surprise and confusion quickened the beat of my heart, leaving me momentarily breathless in the midst of the unexpected gesture.

Gordon held me close as he said, "It's going to be alright. I'm here for you."

I felt soothed by the warmth in his embrace, flustered and yet serene as the tidal waves of guilt began to subside. Time ticked by and I felt the stream of tears that plagued my face dry up.

My face was buried in his shoulder, and I felt truly grateful to have Gordon on my side.

"Aw, well isn't this cute!" A startling voice called out causing Gordon and I to hastily pull away from each other.

I whipped around to see Vulcan, leaning against the opposite wall and smirking. He winked at me.

"N-no! It's not like that-" I started only to be cut off by Vulcan's comical behavior.

He laughed. "I'm teasing! I have eyes, ya know, I saw you with my baby brother."

My face flushed with intense embarrassment, and I instinctively retreated, seeking refuge behind the curtain of my hair. A gentle pat on the top of my head, followed by Vulcan's cordial laugh raised my spirits causing me to laugh as well. Before I knew it all three of us were almost keeling over, cackling at the humor of the situation.

"What are you all laughing about?" Asked a familiar chipper voice followed by a gentle giggle.

Without time to think I felt my body surge towards the voice, embracing its beholder tightly.

"Merlin! You're okay!" I yelled out effervescently.

"Someone's full of energy," Merlin chuckled as he gently wrapped his arms around me.

"I'm as energetic as always!" I exclaimed as I released him from my grasp.

"See? What did I tell you?" I overheard Vulcan snicker as he nudged Gordon with his elbow.

I swiftly turned my head towards Vulcan and my flustered glare pierced his eyes as he grinned back at me. Gordon seemed almost frightened at me in that comedic moment which made Merlin chuckle. However, I found myself reevaluating my emotions about Merlin, only to swiftly dismiss those thoughts due to the embarrassment they brought.

"Anyway," I started, blushing as I turned back to Merlin, "Are you feeling better?"

"Yes, I'm quite alright! No need to worry." Merlin chuckled as he spoke.

"You're up and going sooner than I thought baby brother," Vulcan muttered quietly and delicately smiled to himself.

"I've always been a fighter, as mom has always said." Merlin laughed.

"How is our little sis doing?" Vulcan asked, his tone dropping into seriousness.

"She is as good as new. Just recovering with the help of Mother."

"That's a relief," Vulcan sighed, his shoulders drooping with relief.

"I'm grateful to fate that everything turned out alright in the end," I said, smiling.

"We are here to offer our further support." Gordon chimed in generously.

"I am lucky to have people like you guys by my side," Merlin said.

I felt the facade of cheer fall away, and the gnarled truth reared its baleful head once more.

It's later now. Despite my fears, the time has come.

My cheerful expression faded, remembering that I had to tell Merlin the truth, even if it meant exposing my web of lies and facing the consequences of my deception. The knots of unease tightened in my stomach as I contemplated the impending conversation, grappling with the fear of disappointing him and the uncertainty of how he would react. It was a knot I couldn't simply untangle, a truth I couldn't evade any longer.

"H-hey Merlin?" I started, but stopped, fearful of the upcoming outcome.

"Yes? What's up?" He responded as his glistening eyes enchanted mine.

As he looked at me, waiting, my voice caught in my throat. I looked into his eyes and saw nothing but glittering curiosity.

Vulcan had the right of things. How had I not realized?

Why did I have to realize it now? Now, when I had to hurt him?

I felt my resolve crumble under my feet, my fears rising, that kind, curious look turning pained, angry. Turning away from me and never returning.

My heart couldn't take it. My fear won out. After a long silence, I finally shook my head and said, "It's nothing, never mind."

He tilted his head in confusion before shrugging it off.

I felt a gentle hand rest itself upon my shoulder from behind me followed by a soft whisper in my ear.

"It's alright. Don't push yourself too hard. You'll tell him when the time is right," Gordon said, kindly.

"Anywho, let's all grab something to eat. A midday meal is being prepared for us as we speak." Merlin said, brushing off the confusion.

In unison, we all nodded and trailed after Merlin, progressing down the corridor illuminated by the flickering torchlight. Our journey led us to a grand dining hall, exquisitely adorned in harmony with the carpeted path we had traversed. The elegant decorations resonated with the opulence of the surroundings, creating an atmosphere that combined the allure of mystery with the anticipation of revelations yet to come. The immense window situated opposite bathed the room in the brilliance of the midday sun's radiant beams, resulting in the pure silver plates shimmering in response. I felt as if I were dreaming, unable to believe the surreal beauty and grandeur of the scene before me. The opulent table settings, the play of light and shadow, and the air of elegance combined to create an atmosphere that seemed too enchanting to be real. We were captivated by the alluring ambiance as we glanced around in awe.

"This is beyond incredible, Merlin!" I said gently reaching for his hand.

He cast a brief gaze at my gentle hand before clasping it and speaking, "Even after years of living here, the dining hall still amazes me."

Vulcan playfully nudged Merlin and winked, passing him to take his seat. He then gestured for Gordon to sit on his left, reserving the far left seat for the Queen. Merlin almost seemed to blush as he momentarily scowled at his brother's playful behavior.

"Here follow me, I'll show you to your seat," Merlin said while his expression returned to a peaceful smile.

I nodded in acknowledgment and then offered him a warm smile. As we approached the opposite side of the long table, Merlin graciously pulled a chair out for me before taking a seat beside me.

"Wow, Merlin! What a gentleman!" Vulcan taunted.

"Oh, shut up," Merlin responded, rolling his eyes at his brother's mockery.

My flustered expression at Vulcan's behavior caused Gordon to giggle before forcing a cough to regain his composure.

At that moment, King Arthur, Queen Morgan, and Princess Cerie made their entrance into the room, joining us at the extended table. I turned my attention towards them and offered a gentle smile, feeling a mixture of gratitude and excitement in their presence.

"Good afternoon! I'm glad to see that Cerie is up on her feet!" Merlin said cheerfully as his sister sat beside him.

"I am doing better now thanks to you, brother." Cerie's soft angelic voice spoke out.

King Arthur and Queen Morgan smiled at their son, pleased with the path fate set them on. I gently squeezed Merlin's hand, a heartwarming acknowledgment of the family's reunion. Tears of joy threatened to well up in my eyes, and I blinked them away, truly delighted for their happiness. Everything turned out alright in the end and for that I was thankful. A knock at the door redirected my attention to the current moment. With King Arthur's permission, a maid wheeling a sizable silver cart entered the room, followed by a procession of elegantly attired butlers.

A taller, blonde-haired butler stood a few feet away from the table and announced, "For today's meal, you will be served a delicacy of roasted quail with a side of golden mashed potatoes and roasted sugar snap peas."

The sight of our sumptuous meal being presented on exquisite china plates placed atop sterling silver trays made my mouth water. The exquisite fragrance filled my nostrils as my serving was placed before me, the aroma tantalizing my senses and heightening my anticipation. I gently unfolded my dinner cloth and placed it smoothly across my lap. I eagerly awaited the king's signal to begin our meal, then delicately picked up the larger fork and the gleaming silver knife designated for the main courses. I glanced up once more before taking a small bite of the thinly sliced roasted quail only to notice Vulcan's surprised expression and Gordon's confusion at what to do with his set of silverware. My eyes widened and a flush colored my cheeks as I came to the realization that I shouldn't have been aware of the proper etiquette for using royal silverware. Even Merlin was staring at me, dumbfounded by my proper behavior.

"Lucky guess?" I said sheepishly.

"She is quite the intelligent one isn't she?" King Arthur said, astonished.

"Indeed she is!" Merlin said with an impressed expression believing my claim that it was sheer dumb luck.

After an awkward amount of silence that felt like an eternity, I shifted my gaze to a solitary empty chair positioned at the opposite end of the long table, right across from King Arthur. My curiosity piqued and got the better of me. It was as if that vacant seat held a story of its own, an untold narrative that I yearned to uncover. I couldn't help but wonder who might have sat there before, what discussions had taken place, and whether its emptiness held a deeper meaning. The air seemed charged with unspoken secrets and energy that made me itch to ask, to unravel the mysteries woven into the threads of time and tradition. My mind danced with questions and intrigue, while the grandeur of Camelot's dining hall enveloped us in an air of both opulence and enigma.

"Excuse me, King Arthur?" I started.

"Yes? What is it dear?" He replied softly.

"I-I was wondering who that empty chair belongs to" I started, then shook my head, realizing the question could have come off as disrespectful. "I-I'm sorry I didn't mean to be disrespectful."

"Oh, no my dear! You weren't disrespectful at all! It is alright," he assured. "That chair belongs to the heir to the throne, my eldest son, Talon. He disappeared several weeks ago."

"Oh, my word! That's awful!" I responded.

"Don't worry about it. It's *Talon*, he probably ran off again. He'll be back soon enough," Vulcan said before exchanging agitated glances with his father.

"Let's not show our guests discord. We have a meal cooling before us, yes?" Queen Morgan said tersely. At her side, Cerie flushed with embarrassment, her hand pulling away from the queen's sleeve.

The food was as delicious as it had appeared, and with each bite, my taste buds were treated to an explosion of rich and delectable flavors that coated my senses. It was a culinary experience like nothing I had ever encountered before, yet strangely, it brought to mind memories of my own home. The familiarity of certain spices and textures sparked a rush of nostalgia as if the essence of this foreign feast was reaching out to connect with a part of me that I had left behind. Each mouthful was a journey through the realms of taste and memory, a reminder that even in the grandeur of Camelot, there were echoes of the places I had loved and left behind.

As I savored the flavors on my plate, I couldn't help but feel a twinge of homesickness mixed with gratitude for the opportunity to share in this lavish meal and the stories it whispered through its exquisite presentation.

"Lala," said Merlin's voice carrying me back out of my mind, "would you be interested in walking around Camelot with me?"

"Yes, I would love to! If that's alright with the king and queen that is," I said, glancing over at them in an attempt to prompt them to vocally give their permission.

"Of course you can. You are excused," Queen Morgan nodded.

I smiled before gently placing my dinner cloth neatly on the table. Merlin did the same before standing.

"M'lady." Merlin smiled as he offered his hand to assist me to my feet.

I giggled as I rushed out of the room beside him, hand still in his.

It was almost as if we were elegantly dancing as we went down the corridor and towards the front gate.

"Wait, Lala. There is something I need to show you first," Merlin started as we ducked into another corridor leading left of the front gate.

I felt a rush of excitement flow through my veins as we reached another set of large heavy walnut doors. Merlin suddenly stopped and stood facing me, gazing deeply into my eyes. I felt my face once again grow flush as his enchanted demeanor cast its kind radiance upon me.

"Now, close your eyes," Merlin requested.

"Wait, why?" I asked with both confusion and nervousness in my voice.

"Just trust me," he said as he gently touched his rough hand to my soft cheek causing me to blush even more.

"Okay, I trust you," I smiled as I allowed my eyelids to flutter shut.

My heart was pounding in my chest as if I had started sprinting in a race. I felt the excitement continue to consume my essence as every second passed. I heard the loud creaking of the opening doors that stood before me as a familiar hand grasped onto mine and gently pulled me forward. I took a deep breath in as the smell of lignin, hexanal, and dust filled my nose, causing me to let out a small sneeze. I heard Merlin chuckle and I giggled alongside him.

"Okay, open your eyes," Merlin said, cheerfully.

I slowly opened my adjusting eyes as the small sting of light entered my retinas. To my amazement, a huge circular room with dozens of bookshelves filled to the ceiling with novels and scrolls enchanted the atmosphere around me. I stared in disbelief at the endless knowledge-filled chamber that we had entered. I felt as if I had awoken into a special kind of dream. Merlin's laughter snapped me back to reality as I realized my jaw had dropped and a faint gasp had escaped me.

"I take it you enjoy our library?" Merlin asked, rhetorically.

"Merlin, it's beautiful," I stammered, still trying to distinguish fact from fiction.

"I thought you'd enjoy it," he said with a soft chuckle.

I scanned around the room, eyeing the beautiful spines of the leatherback tomes that rested flawlessly in alphabetical order by genre along the bookshelves. Stepping deeper into the grandeur of Camelot's royal library, my breath was caught in my throat as my gaze swept over the towering bookshelves that seemed to stretch into eternity. Sunlight streamed through the tall windows, illuminating the intricate spines of countless tomes, their gold-embossed titles shimmering like a treasure trove of knowledge waiting to be uncovered.

The air carried the scent of ancient parchment and the faint whisper of untold stories. I felt a surge of reverence as Merlin and I walked along the polished marble floor, my fingertips grazing the bindings of the books as if they held secrets I longed to unravel. Each shelf was a portal to a different world, offering realms of magic, adventure, and wisdom. The vastness of the library felt like a living entity, a repository of the accumulated wisdom of generations past, a testament to the unbreakable bond between the elves and the written word. As we explored the labyrinthine aisles, I imagined myself embarking on countless journeys, my mind free to roam and discover. This sanctuary of thought, with its towering arches and hushed reverence, whispered of the endless possibilities that awaited those who dared to open a book and let their imagination soar.

That was until my gaze fell upon a wall filled with the education and history of the different regions within our realm called Azethe. My curiosity peaked which Merlin seemed to have noticed as he placed his rough hand on my bare shoulder.

"Ah, yes. Those scrolls hold everything we know about the other races, populations, and even the religions that those races and populations follow."

"Is this how you learned about historical events?"

"Indeed it is," he responded, an air of pride about him. It was certainly a collection to be proud of.

"Wait," I said, narrowing my eyes, "you mentioned other races and populations. We didn't have much knowledge about others, beyond our neighboring eastern wood elf sister colony. Do you think there might be other elvish colonies?"

"Yes, there are many other elvish colonies similar to yours! There are also many different kinds of elves as well," Merlin explained with enthusiasm.

I felt curiosity grasp control of my consciousness as questions began to spiral in my mind. As a child, I was taught about the history of my own colony and the importance of solely focusing on my own people. Although learning this had its benefits, it left me unaware of the life that existed around us. The thought of other elvish beings exhilarated me with a new deep desire for adventure and education.

"Would it be alright if I asked you to teach me a little about the others?" I asked sheepishly. I couldn't contain my curiosity, nor the thrill of exhilaration at the thought of other elves.

"Of course m'lady," he replied, bowing with a flourish.

I smiled as he gestured for me to follow him to a small squarish walnut table. He graciously pulled out a wooden chair for me and then took a seat across from where I was seated. With a wink he swiftly flung his arm outward before allowing it to gently fall back to his side, and, to my surprise, a book hovered into his magic-encased hand.

"Let's see here," Merlin mused as he began flipping through pages.

I gazed at him with awe-filled eyes as the enchanting atmosphere swept me into a vivid daydream. My emotions towards him were both so clear yet uncertain. I felt as if my soul had been once again set free as a delightful euphoric bliss fluttered within my chest. It was these moments with him that made me feel truly alive and full of vibrant colors and hues. My life was a mosaic and I was but a tile.

"Let's start with the Western colonies," Merlin began as he turned over the book so that I could see the roughly drawn elvish figure with gingerbread skin and amaranth-colored hair, "These are the Sundrop Elves. Known for having a deep connection with the solar periods, the Sundrop Elves reside in hot sandy areas, such as the badlands and deserts of Quenntebis. These elves harvest the power of the sun through the use of fire-style druid magic."

"Wow, that sounds incredible! They use magic similarly to us, but at the same time it's still a bit different."

He smiled at me. "Listen to this. The Solus dance is the most powerful Sundrop elvish spell where a sole individual connects themself directly to the blazing power of the sun," Merlin read, "It is said that the skin of these elves can reach a scorching heat of twelve hundred degrees Celsius." He glanced at me, then added, "That's two thousand... one hundred eight... no, ninety degrees Fahrenheit for you."

I laughed. "You remembered." I'd already thought it was hot when it was over a thousand, but over two thousand. "That's incredible."

As the newfound knowledge settled into my mind, I was struck by an awe that felt almost electric. It was as if a hidden door had swung open, revealing a realm of understanding that had previously eluded me. The pieces of the puzzle clicked into place, forming a tapestry of insight that expanded my horizons and rewired my perception of the world. With each revelation, my sense of wonder grew, and I marveled at the intricacies of the universe that had been laid bare before me. It was a humbling reminder of the vastness of human discovery, a testament to the boundless potential for growth and enlightenment that exists within the realm of knowledge.

"That's hotter than molten lava," Merlin replied, seemingly intrigued by his newly gained knowledge.

"If that's how hot their skin gets, I'm terrified to know how hot their actual *flames* get," I commented, inquisitively.

"It doesn't say in this book, unfortunately," Merlin said, skimming through the text on the thick papyrus pages.

"That's a shame," I sighed.

"Someday I'll take you to Quenntebis and you can ask them," Merlin suggested, light-heartedly.

"Really?" I couldn't help but be excited by the prospect of spending more time with him.

"I promise," he swore with a silly bow that caused me to giggle.

"So long as you remind me to never anger a Sundrop elf," I joked.

Once again, the captivation of a peaceful daydream held my mind hostage. I imagined myself holding hands with Merlin walking along the desert sands and joking amongst ourselves. With a heart brimming with anticipation, I couldn't help but smile at the thought of embarking on an adventure alongside the person I held dearest. The mere idea of setting out together, forging new paths, and creating shared memories, ignited a spark of excitement within my soul. Imagining our laughter echoing through unexplored landscapes, our camaraderie strengthening with every challenge we overcame, filled me with a sense of exhilaration. The prospect of weaving our stories together, side by side, was a promise of boundless discovery and an affirmation of the profound connection we shared.

For a fleeting moment, I felt an emotion I wasn't familiar with. My face began to become hot, and I quickly shook my head in an attempt to bring myself back to the present.

"Let's move on, shall we?" Merlin inquired.

I nodded as he flipped through a few more pages before stopping and smiling exuberantly.

"Lala, look! This is very interesting," Merlin exclaimed as he faced the book towards me once more.

I examined the beige pages, finding them full of peculiar images and various paragraphs until I saw the heading on the page: "Frostfire Elves". I vaguely recalled hearing about these northern elves as a child whilst enrolled in kinder school. Merlin seemed to notice this, causing his face to light up like a festival orb.

"You've heard of Frostfire Elves before?" Merlin asked, a smile spreading across his face.

"Indeed I have, back when I was young," I replied, matching the energy he presented, "Though, I don't remember much."

"Well, according to this tome, these elves live in the northern hemisphere," Merlin recited.

"If I remember correctly, I believe they live near the Boreal Nymphs and the Winter Elementals," I replied, a hint of uncertainty in fear that my memories were incorrect.

"You're absolutely right," Merlin said, passionately, before continuing to read. "It says here that, when enraged,

Frostfire elves can emit a vengeful blue flame that can get as cold as negative two hundred degrees Celsius!" He looked up for a moment, toward the ceiling, then added, "Or… negative three hundred twenty-eight degrees Fahrenheit."

"Isn't that colder than that liquid stuff humans use for dermatological purposes?" I asked, cautiously.

"Indeed it is! It's called liquid nitrogen," Merlin informed me before continuing to internally skim through the paragraphs before him.

"That's incredibly freezing," I said, wide-eyed and bewildered by the powerful force these elves possess.

"Not only that, their bodies can get as cold as negative seventy-eight degrees Celsius. That's as cold as dry ice," Merlin declared, shocked by the information he was reading.

"But how cold is it in Fahrenheit?" I asked, excited. I didn't have something like the temperature of dry ice memorized, and Merlin was distracted by his shock.

"Oh, sorry," he said. "It's one hundred… eight? Maybe nine."

"Oh my goodness," I replied, perplexed and fascinated.

"Now those are the elves I would love to meet and question," he said with a wink.

"Someday maybe I'll take you there," I said with a sweet smile.

"I'd like that very much," he replied.

I smiled at him shyly pulling a stray strand of hair behind my ear as my cheeks became flushed and rosy. My emotions fluttered and there was a split second where I almost dared to press my soft lips against his, but I restrained myself.

His bewitching voice pulled me from my inhibitions and refocused my attention on the tome that he continued to flip through.

"There are a whole lot more in here too! Plutonic Elves, Mermaids, Sirens, Vampires, Ghosts, Trolls, Goblins, Pixies, various types of Dwarves, different types of Golems, and so much more," Merlin's voice was full of life and energy which caused me to laugh out of happiness and joy.

"Who would have thought knowledge could be so empowering?" I rhetorically asked.

With a loud gasp, Merlin jumped from his seat and wrapped his arm around me, placing the book in front of both of us.

"Look at this! Moonshine elves that derive power from the moon itself." He spoke with the excitement of a small puppy playing with a newly obtained toy.

"It says they're masters at illusions and sleepful song," I recited to Merlin as I admired the pointy ears on a sketch that lay beside the writing.

"Wow, these elves have pewter gray skin and cloud silver hair."

"That's so amazing," I replied, cherishing the jocund memories we were making together.

"Oh! This is interesting." He had flipped the page, revealing a heading that read: "Starfall Elves".

"I've never heard of this kind of elf before."

"It says here that not much is known about these elves, so that doesn't surprise me," Merlin replied, narrowing his eyes in befuddlement.

"It says here that they keep to themselves and are never seen outside their territory," I said, raising my eyebrows at the mystifying nature of the pages I read.

"That almost sounds cult-like," Merlin replied, prudently.

"They live in the crater of a fallen meteorite upon an undisclosed mountain…" I started before trailing off.

My eyes widened with disbelief as I noticed that the previously sketched image had been deeply scratched out beyond recognition. Many questions filled my mind and demanded answers I had not received.

"That's odd. I wonder who vandalized this page," Merlin said, both confused and concerned as he looked at the damaged page in my hands.

The sudden creak of doors opening caused Merlin and I to jump defensively before quickly remembering that we hadn't a need for worry.

"Did I walk into you two making out or something?" Vulcan asked, snickering.

"No! It's not-" Merlin stammered, embarrassingly.

I felt my face erupt as a cherry-red hue plagued my cheeks.

"Oh I see, you haven't confessed to each other yet. How cute," Vulcan mocked as he walked into the room and pulled a chair up beside us, straddling it and leaning his arms on the chair back.

I tugged a strand of hair and pulled it in front of my face in an attempt to hide my flustered expression, but my behavior only caused his grin to expand across his face. My gaze shifted to Merlin whose face was bright red with embarrassment. He was nervously fidgeting with his hands and biting the inside of his cheek. It almost made me smile as I found his shy behavior to be adorable.

"Weren't you two supposed to be heading into town?" Vulcan asked, a little more serious than before.

"Oh, crap! I completely forgot." Merlin exclaimed.

"We got a little sidetracked. I wanted to learn more about the other elvish colonies and I adore reading so Merlin wanted to surprise me," I explained.

"Surprise you, ay?" Vulcan mocked, childishly with a wink.

"Not like that," Merlin said, rolling his eyes.

I blushed realizing what Vulcan was insinuating and tried to hide behind my hair once more. Vulcan laughed and patted Merlin on the shoulder before standing up to walk deeper into the library.

"I'm only teasing. I'm gonna be here for a while if either of you need anything," Vulcan said as he strolled away.

Merlin and I turned to face each other, both of us still blushing. He gently took my hand and began to gently tug me towards the doors which we had entered.

"Come on, let's go before all the popular merchandise gets purchased," he said, cheerfully, "I would like you to experience the full glory of my home!"

I gaily smiled and gladly followed him down the outstretched corridor and out the front gate. I was excited and carefree when I was with him. I felt as light as a feather, untied and free. Even as we walked the streets of Camelot I couldn't shake the enchanting emotion that enveloped my consciousness. Vibrant hues of color painted the scene around us, accompanied by an array of delightful scents that wafted through the air. It was as if we had entered a realm of sensory wonder, where every step was a journey into a new dimension of colors and fragrances. The town remained just as lively as before, with the joyful laughter of children playing, filling my ears and causing an uncontrollable smile to spread across my face. It was heartwarming to witness the simple yet genuine moments of happiness that surrounded us.

"I brought some gold with me so that I can show you the best items in Camelot," Merlin said, passionately.

With that, he took the lead and guided me from one shop booth to another, immersing us in a whirlwind of bustling activity and vibrant displays. Each counter was a treasure trove of distinct items and delectable foods, capturing my attention and filling my eyes with wonder as I marveled at the diversity on display. With each kiosk we stopped at, I felt more and more amazed at the lifestyle of human beings. Their warm gestures and friendly interactions made me feel almost as if I belonged there, among the bustling energy of the town. As I navigated through the lively market, my senses were inundated with an array of new stimuli, filling me with awe and delight. The vibrant colors, tantalizing aromas, and lively chatter of the people around me created a symphony of sensations that was both exhilarating and invigorating. At one booth, Merlin caught me staring in awe at a small azure teardrop amulet. Without a second thought, he handed the vermillion-eyed shopkeeper three gold pieces and gently clasped the amulet around my neck. With a beaming smile, my cheeks flushed with gratitude as I expressed my heartfelt thanks for his generosity.

"It's aquamarine. You have a good eye," Merlin smiled at me.

"It's absolutely beautiful!" I exclaimed.

"A beautiful pendant for a beautiful young lady," he smiled at me warmly, and I felt my face burn with infatuation.

I was left utterly speechless by the graceful manner in which Merlin conducted himself before me. I yearned to convey my profound emotions through a tender kiss at that very moment, yet I held back due to my apprehension of his potential disapproval. As quickly as it started, my daydream ended with the affable sound of his gentle voice.

"Lala, have you ever tried ice cream before?" Merlin asked, glancing over at a local stand.

"Can't say I have. I don't even know what it is." I answered, giggling at myself.

"Wait here for a minute," he said as he rushed through the fluctuating crowd of people.

My laughter resonated through the air as I found myself thoroughly entertained by his enthusiastic demeanor. It was a heartwarming sight that brought a genuine smile to my lips. I let my eyes wander around me, admiring the chatter and its beholders.

"So this is how humans live. It's so wonderful." I happily muttered to myself as contentment embraced me with her warm arms.

Out of the blue, I sensed two hands gently covering my eyes, and a giggle escaped my lips as I instinctively assumed it was Merlin.

"Merlin, cut it out," I laughed until the air was filled with silence, slaying my laughter on the spot. "Seriously Merlin, knock it off, it isn't funny anymore."

"Guess again," said a familiar voice before I felt my body lunge backward causing a silent yelp to escape my paralyzed vocal cords.

The hands shifted from veiling my eyes to silencing my mouth, and my hazy vision cleared, revealing the almost concealed countenances of my childhood friend and my sister.

"I knew it was you. I'd recognize that voice anywhere," Gwen said almost emotionlessly before uncovering my mouth, knowing I wouldn't scream.

"Gwen?! Freya?!" I exclaimed dumbfoundedly, "How did you- When did you- What?!"

"Princess Ilana Lanthir, you are under arrest by the elvish King Îdhron Lanthir's orders," Gwen said sternly.

"You are to be returned to Aefaradiron at once and punished accordingly." Freya chimed in before tightly binding my hands behind my back with thick rope.

"W-wait! I have friends here I need to tell-" I started but was cut off by Freya's aggressive voice.

"Ilana, you scared us half to death. We didn't know where you went or if you were kidnapped or worse…" Freya said grimly.

"It's in your best interest to come quietly to not attract attention. We owe you nothing. We are leaving right now, end of discussion," Gwen said with authority.

I struggled, knowing that I had to get away from them until a sudden voice caused me to freeze in place.

"Get your hands off of her!" Merlin let out a low growl, letting two ice cream cones fall to the ground as he readied himself for an impending attack.

"Princess Ilana is coming with us whether you want her to or not," Gwen scowled as she unsheathed her copper-bladed dagger.

Merlin's stance changed as confusion filled his eyes and he said, "Princess? Ilana?"

He looked at my sorrow-filled expression and his confused eyes quickly became cold with betrayal.

"You lied to me," said Merlin as he clenched his fists with rage. "And after all we've been through."

"Merlin, I-" I began.

"Y'know what? No, I don't want to hear it from you. I can't believe after all this time, you couldn't *trust* me."

"Merlin, I wanted to tell you. I even tried to. I just didn't want to hurt you..." I said through tears.

"You didn't want to hurt me?! Well look where that got you, Lala or Ilana or whoever you are!" Merlin yelled as his eyebrows lowered and his jaw clenched.

My sister began pulling me with her out of the alley towards a secluded back path out of Camelot and all I could do was mouth the words "I'm sorry" before sorrow consumed me and tears plagued my once happy face. As I was swept away, I watched Merlin, and he watched me.

He just watched.

CHAPTER 7

Everything around me had changed as her web of lies unraveled. There is no greater misery than the pain of betrayal bestowed upon you by the person you love the most. The weight of betrayal settled on my shoulders like a leaden cloak, its burden nearly suffocating me as the truth unfurled before my eyes. The realization that Lala, the young elvish woman I had come to trust and confide in, had lied to me about her identity, cut deep into my heart like a dagger. She couldn't even trust me with her name. Ilana. The memories of our shared moments, the laughter and conversations we had exchanged, now felt tainted by the shadow of deception. My mind churned with a tumult of emotions, each one a separate blade driving into my psyche. I felt anger, not just at her, but at myself for allowing my naive mind to be taken in by her ruse. But beneath the anger, a gnawing hurt festered—a sense of abandonment that stung more deeply than I cared to admit. The connection we had formed, based on what I believed to be the truth, now stood shattered, leaving me adrift in a sea of doubt and disappointment. It wasn't just the lie itself that wounded me, but the sense of loneliness that gnawed at the very foundation of trust I held dear. The pain was a visceral ache, a reminder that even in a world of magic, the wounds inflicted by those closest to us could cut the deepest. As I grappled with the turmoil within, a part of me wished for the power to turn back time, to rewrite the time we had shared, searching for clues I might have missed. But time continued to flow forward, and all that remained was the raw sting of betrayal, a wound that would take time to heal if it ever truly could. After a short while, even time and emotion grew grim and cold, ceasing to exist to me as I plummeted into an unfamiliar abyss. Time after time the faint knocking at my door followed by voices echoed in the back of my mind, but all I could do was lay in quietness. The silence pierced my ears as the echoes of thoughts reverberated within my mind. Nothing could pull me out of this despair. Nothing.

"Merlin, you have to come out and eat something or at least have some water," a familiar, gentle voice called out.

A sigh followed with the fidgeting of a lock nearly liberated me from my lifeless daze and my bedroom door creaked open as Gordon anxiously entered.

"Merlin, please. It's been two days since anyone has seen or heard from you…" Gordon said worriedly.

I couldn't respond. I was still entranced by my own darkness. His words made sounds that I heard, but I couldn't grasp their meaning whilst in this empty void I found myself in. The static in my own mind grew louder, an overwhelming cacophony that drowned out a coherent thought. Like a dense fog, it cloaked audible words, rendering them muffled and fragmented. Each attempt to speak was met with a wall of confusion, the torrent of mental noise rendering my voice powerless, trapped in the labyrinth of my racing thoughts. Frustration and helplessness gripped me as I struggled to break through the barrier, to find a way to articulate the chaos that reigned within.

"Talk to me, lad." Gordon pleaded as he gently sat beside me at my bedside.

Alas, there was still nothing. Gordon sighed, preparing himself to leave me alone with my anguish until he clenched his fists and began sobbing. The dripping sound of his tears raining from his helpless eyes onto his fists and brown leggings was able to awaken me from my foggy state.

"I just don't... I don't know what to do I-" said Gordon, choking on his words as he helplessly wept.

In that moment I was able to sympathize with his forlorn composure. I allowed a few tears of my own to be shed and I slowly sat up on my bedside next to Gordon, wrapping my arm around him in an attempt to provide comfort. He winced, surprised by my sudden ability to react.

"I never meant to scare anyone. I just feel so... empty inside." I said in a grim monotone voice.

"I know, but I also know that she never meant to hurt you." Gordon whimpered, "She did it to protect herself. How was she supposed to know we were safe?"

"She should have come clean though," I replied gloomily.

"She was trying to. She was scared. She didn't want to hurt you." Gordon sniffled. "Everything that she has done up to this point, she has done for you. Knowing that, do you really think she wanted to keep this from you?"

"Deep down I know that, but it still hurts like hell," I said, grasping my chest tightly.

"Do you think she ever wanted you to find out this way?" Gordon asked.

"I-" I started before looking down at my hands.

"Merlin, Lala is in love with you. She cares for you above everything else and she would never give up on you," he said compassionately.

I blushed. I hadn't truly realized her emotions for me were that strong and to think I thought she didn't trust me. An image of her sweet smile that stretched across her rosy cheeks captivated my mind, etching itself as a cherished memory. In that fleeting moment, the warmth of her joy radiated through her expression, leaving an indelible mark on my heart. The purity of that smile spoke of innocence, happiness, and the beauty of simple moments shared. It was a reminder that amid life's challenges, there are still moments of unadulterated happiness to treasure and hold close. I realized how foolish I had been to get so angry at her. I was speechless.

"I know it has wounded you, but are you really going to allow her to be stolen away from you?" Gordon squeaked as his crying finally began to stop. "Are you really about to lose her because of a mistake she made?"

I went silent. I had been selfish to allow my dubiousness to consume me whilst she continued to grow further and further away from me.

I let out a sigh and said, "I've been selfish. I need to get her back and then we can resolve this like adults."

"Feeling emotions isn't being selfish. It's alright to be in pain and it's alright to cry, but you can't allow it to consume your whole being." Gordon reassured me.

I wiped the tears from my face as I slowly stood from my bedside, followed shortly by Gordon. Truthfully I knew I loved Lala, I was just too afraid to admit it. Knowing she loved me in return filled my body and soul with a new kind of power, a strength that transcended the physical realm. It was a force that surged through my veins, igniting a fire within me to be the best version of myself, to protect and cherish her, and to build a future together filled with shared dreams and endless devotion. With her love as my anchor, I felt unbreakable, capable of facing any challenge that life might throw our way. In that fleeting moment of revelation, the world around me seemed to shift and blur, as if the very fabric of reality was altered by the intensity of my emotions. A rush of warmth surged from the depths of my heart, spreading through every fiber of my being like sunlight breaking through a stormy sky. The air crackled with newfound energy, and every sensation was heightened as if I had unlocked a secret dimension of existence. The mere thought of her ignited a symphony of butterflies in my stomach, their delicate wings carrying me to heights I had never known before. The world became a canvas painted with vibrant hues of joy, and the simplest things, like the sound of her laughter or the touch of her hand, held a profound significance. It was as if love had illuminated my soul, casting aside doubts and fears, and I felt invincible, ready to face any challenge that came my way. In that exhilarating moment, the realization that I was in love with the person I held dearest transformed my world into a place of boundless wonder and endless possibilities. I felt a strange kindling fire ignite inside my heart and I felt a new kind of determination take hold of me.

"Together?" Gordon asked with a shy smile, holding his hand out to me.

"Let's go get Lala back," I responded, shaking his hand.

From then on I swore to myself that I would protect her no matter the cost. She meant the world to me and I was too arrogant to admit it. It was time for me to set aside my flaws and face fate head-on. With unwavering determination, I gazed into the depths of my heart and made a solemn vow to myself. The fierce fire of devotion burned within me, igniting a promise that transcended all boundaries. I swore to safeguard Lala, the one I truly loved, beyond measure, to stand as an unyielding shield against the storms of life, no matter the cost. In that moment, I cast aside any notion of sacrifice or hardship, fully embracing the weight of responsibility that came with this self-imposed duty. The echoes of my vow reverberated through my very soul, intertwining my fate with hers, and I knew that I would navigate the darkest abyss and face the fiercest challenges to ensure their safety and happiness. It was a vow etched in my heart, a declaration of my unwavering commitment to protect her, to keep her light aglow amid life's shadows.

"I'm coming Lala, just hold on a little longer." I thought to myself with determination.

We hurried out of my bedroom to alert my parents of our upcoming journey. We had to devise a method to catch up to her swiftly, recognizing that traveling on foot wouldn't provide the speed we required – a realization that was shared between both of us.

"Where are you two off to in such a hurry? Merlin, I'm glad to see you've stopped sulking like a child." Vulcan's voice echoed down the long hallway.

"Shut it, Vulcan. We are going to save Lala." I retorted.

"Oh you mean that little lying elf princess? I don't think so. You aren't going anywhere." Vulcan yelled spitefully.

"She made some mistakes and I did too. I want to fix it." I said as I slowly came to a halt and turned around to face him.

"She betrayed you. Plus she is a wood elf. Her kind isn't welcomed here because they are manipulating fiends. You of all people should have realized that by now." Vulcan said bitterly.

I heard Gordon grit his teeth as he stepped forward. His face contorted in anger as he snapped his fingers, unleashing a burst of emerald green magic that surged from his fingertips, simultaneously materializing his elvish ears from thin air.

"Don't ever…" Gordon said quietly which quickly erupted into a vengeful scream, "insult my kind like that ever again!"

His green eyes began glowing as they widened with malice, revealing the whites of his eyes, and his eyebrows lowered to a steep downward curve, coating his face in shadows. I experienced an unfamiliar vindictive power surrounding me, causing a shiver of fear to course through my body. I could sense that Vulcan perceived it as well, as his expression swiftly shifted from bitterness to unease in a matter of seconds.

"H-hey, wait a minute let's talk about this." Vulcan stammered.

"You talk about how horrible my race is while you disgusting humans rely on strength and brute force to solve your problems." Gordon fulminated as he advanced closer and closer to Vulcan.

"Gordon, please stop," I murmured. It turned out to be a little too quiet since he continued to progress forward toward my petrified brother without hesitation.

"How pathetic you barbaric humans are!"

"He's completely lost it… He's gone mad!" Vulcan cried out in terror as he stumbled backward.

I watched in horror as Gordon drew his hand back and a pine-green bow of light appeared in front of him followed by a quiver that shined in the same luminescence as the bow. This magic that he conjured was different and colder than before. He had been completely consumed by the darkness, his features contorted into a twisted expression that sent chills down my spine. I had to find a way to break through to the real Gordon, the Gordon I'd come to know and befriend. What stood before me was merely a twisted replica, a mirror image of the kind-hearted young half-elf that saved Lala and me from Alastor's grasp.

"Gordon stop!" I howled, but it was no use.

I couldn't get through to him with words. I threw my body forward as I recklessly ran at Gordon and tackled him, pinning him to the ground.

"Let go of me!" He screeched wrathfully.

"Gordon, snap out of it! You have to calm down!" I yelled, struggling to terminate his thrashing movements.

"Get a hold of yourself, kid!" Vulcan shouted as he knelt down to firmly slap Gordon across the face in a final attempt to drag him back to his senses.

To my surprise, it worked. Gordon's expression went from tainted by animosity to consumed by consternation. I slowly got off of him, allowing him to sit up. His head dropped and tears smeared his throbbing cheek as his eyes widened once more, but this time with pure terror of who he had become in that abhorrent moment. He hastily drew his hand to his mouth to hold himself back from regurgitating his stomach contents.

"Did I... Was that... Who..." He stammered in disbelief.

"It's alright now. I'm sorry for what I said. It had no merit and it was disingenuous." Vulcan said remorsefully before widening his eyes in shock and concern.

As Vulcan's words ceased, Gordon's eyes rolled into his head and his lifeless body crumpled to the ground with a small thud. Urgently, I leaned over to assess his pulse, which appeared stable except for his heightened heart rate, a lingering effect of the adrenaline surge that was slowly subsiding. Beads of sweat adorned his flushed face, prompting me to lift my hand and gently touch his forehead to gauge his temperature.

"He's burning up," I said.

"Will he be okay?" Vulcan asked worriedly.

"He'll be fine. He just needs some rest and a cool cloth on his forehead. That took a lot out of him." I responded reassuringly.

Vulcan nodded as he gently lifted Gordon from the ground before he said, "I'm going to take him to the guest room while we wait for him to wake. I would hate to leave him on the filthy ground like this."

"Agreed," I said, and we began down the hallway.

Truthfully, I was worried about Gordon after his outburst. Were elvish emotions really that powerful? And, if so, then I couldn't begin to imagine the hell Lala was enduring. I held onto the belief that she had the strength to endure a bit more suffering as we focused our attention on Gordon's condition.

"Hang in there Lala, we will come for you soon. I promise." I said aloud.

"Still worried about your little girlfriend, huh?" Vulcan said as he entered the guest room and gently laid Gordon on the soft quilted mattress.

I felt my face tingle as I started to blush and I said sheepishly, "Of course, I'm still worried about her. She means everything to me."

"Yeah, yeah, I know," said Vulcan as he rolled his eyes.

"On a more serious note, you can't say things about other races like you did back there. It was cruel." I said as I pulled a small cloth from my messenger bag along with a small flask of water.

"It was a heat of the moment thing. I was still fuming about how Ilana lied to you. You've never fallen in love before her and I know what both love and heartbreak can do to a man. You're my little brother. I look out for you, y'know." He replied diffidently.

"Wow, that must've taken a lot of guts to say to my face." I joked as I poured a little water on the cloth.

"Heh, you know it. When you're an old timer like me you'll understand the importance of showing a little love to your siblings." He chuckled as he winked at me.

"Oldtimer? Slow down there cowboy, you aren't that old yet." I laughed, laying the cool cloth on Gordon's forehead as I spoke.

We both laughed. As much as my brother irritated me at times, I cared for him deeply and would do anything for him.

"Seriously though, I deeply regret what I said about the elvish race as well as what I said about Ilana. I'm sorry." Vulcan said remorsefully as he turned to look me directly in the eyes.

"All is forgiven, as long as you promise not to do it again," I said, smiling at him.

"I promise. I won't behave like that again." He replied.

A soft grunt diverted our attention back to Gordon who was breathing heavily whilst still unconscious. It seemed that his fever was being combated by his own body's defenses. Vulcan sat on the edge of the mattress beside him and gently grasped his hand.

"Y'know," Vulcan said, gently rubbing his thumb across the back of Gordon's smooth motionless hand, "he reminds me of you when you were younger." He glanced over to me, then back to Gordon. "You both have that same shimmer in your eyes."

"Is that so?" I said, smirking.

"What? Why are you smiling?" He asked confusedly before realizing my intentions.

Blushing deeply, he attempted to avert his gaze from me, clearly embarrassed. I softly jabbed his side with my elbow as I sat down beside him.

"I won't poke you too much about it. Your secret's safe with me, Vulcan." I said soothingly.

"Thank you. I'll confront my emotions, and our parents for that matter, when I'm ready." He replied nervously.

"No rush. Don't push yourself."

"Who's rushing?" he asked, gently sliding his hand away from Gordon's.

"Now I understand why Talon was the ladies' man," I joked, hoping to prod a laugh out of him and ease the worried furrow on his brow.

"Though, I am the handsome one out of us," he replied, smug and overconfident as ever.

"Hey now, that's pushing the line a little," I responded with a laugh causing him to laugh alongside me.

I gently patted his back before allowing my mind to take hold of my attention once more. I thought back to the agonizing moment when Lala was taken from Camelot, the surge of anger and profound sorrow that had coursed through me. The memory replayed vividly in my mind, a relentless reminder of my powerlessness in the face of injustice. Every image, every emotion, etched deeply into my soul, driving me to find a way to bring her back, to right the wrong that had been done. The intensity of my determination was matched only by the depth of my heartache, a swirling vortex of conflicting emotions that propelled me forward despite the odds stacked against me. I recalled the scene vividly, how I had witnessed the elvish girl lift Lala onto a chestnut stallion, tethered to another woman of her kind, both following her palomino horse. I pondered how we could possibly catch up to Lala when they were already mounted on horseback. Even with horses ourselves, we wouldn't reach a fast enough speed to catch them before they reached their homeland. A sense of hopelessness hung in the air, casting a shadow over our uncertain situation. I felt the weight of helplessness chaining me down, an oppressive force that left me struggling for control.

"Hello? Earth to Merlin?" Vulcan interrupted as he waved his hand in front of my face to seize my attention.

"Huh? What's up?" I inquired.

"What's going on in that little head of yours? You seem troubled." His voice trembled with worry as he asked, his eyes reflecting a deep concern and sorrow.

"Well, I'm worried about how we will catch up to Lala. They have a fair distance from us, and they are on horseback. I just don't know how to catch up, or if it is even possible." I said solemnly as I grasped my chin with my hand, resting my index finger on my bottom lip.

"I would have to pull some strings, but I may have a solution. Just leave it to me," Vulcan said enthusiastically with a charismatic grin.

A sudden groan refocused our attention on Gordon who was finally coming to. His eyes weakly scanned the room as he attempted to gather his bearings. I could see the confusion and exhaustion etched on his face, a testament to the ordeal he had endured.

"What happened?" Gordon asked, perplexed by the strange unfamiliar atmosphere.

"You got yourself all worked up and fainted," Vulcan said softly.

"How are you feeling?" I asked.

"I feel sluggish, but I'll be fine," Gordon replied before he slowly began to sit up.

"Woah! Take it easy, bud. Don't overdo it." Vulcan said, cradling Gordon's back for stability as his body began to lean backward.

"I'm fine, thank you," Gordon replied kindly as he steadied himself. "We have to get to Lala before it's too late."

"Gordon, you need to worry about your well-being first. Once we are convinced that you're alright, then we can go after Ilana." Vulcan said sternly.

"I have to agree with my brother. You know I want to get her back as much as you do, but we need to prioritize your health right now." I uttered with concern, a hint of sadness gleaming in my eyes.

"I promise you that I can handle it. Besides, I have you guys to look out for me." Gordon reassured us before throwing his legs over the bedside and hoisting himself to his feet.

"If you say so," muttered Vulcan, his worry for Gordon still evident in his tone. "I'll assist you for the time being. You both should follow me. Oh, and I don't think it would be best to tell mother and father about this. They are already furious with the elvish race because of an alliance dispute that happened decades ago and now with the spiteful rumors that have been going around after what Princess Ilana did to you... It would be best to avoid conflict."

"Do you know what this alliance dispute was about?" I asked confusedly.

"I can answer that," Gordon interjected before Vulcan could respond. "The humans wished to form an alliance with the elves, who were all bound as one kingdom. The elves were powerful at the time and could hold their own. That was before the humans took that away from us."

"Hold on, that's not what I heard! I heard that the elves wanted power for themselves and betrayed the humans in an attempt to gain more territory and enslave our race!" Vulcan yelled aggressively before taking a deep breath to calm himself down.

Gordon glared before also releasing tension with his breath. I felt the hostility grow within the atmosphere and I chose to stay quiet and listen in fear of angering both parties involved.

"A small group of assassins invaded us and murdered dozens of our people under the cover of night. Not only that, but they stole valuable goods from us and set fire to our kingdom." Gordon's grief-filled voice quivered as he spoke, "Witnesses recalled seeing humans wearing cloaks with their royal symbol embroidered on the back of the hoods before they escaped into the shadows. The humans betrayed us, robbed us, murdered our civilians, and burned our houses to the ground. How the hell could we forgive them for that?!"

"What?! Bullshit! Your kind stole from and attacked us!" Vulcan shouted, unable to contain his anger. He took a deep breath before continuing, trying to make sense of the chaos. "But—wait—didn't the items you offered during the negotiations go missing right before all this? And there were rumors about elven officials—those who were pushing hardest for peace—being assassinated days before? How convenient for the ones who opposed the treaty, isn't it?"

Gordon's eyes narrowed in suspicion, his anger mingling with confusion. Vulcan pressed on, his voice steadying. "On our side, too, goods disappeared without a trace. People who spoke out for peace were found dead, and the same night, humans in royal cloaks were spotted attacking your people. But who exactly were they?"

He looked Gordon in the eye. "What if someone else wanted to make sure that peace never happened?"

Gordon hesitated, though his grief remained palpable. "And you expect me to believe this?"

"I don't expect anything. But think about it, Gordon. Why would we jeopardize an alliance both our kingdoms desperately need? Someone's playing us both. And they're doing it in plain sight."

Knowing that this situation was getting out of hand I said, "The past is the past, even if it was grim. How about we focus on reuniting forces to better our futures?"

"It's not going to be easy, but if it's possible, it would be the best for both of our races," Gordon said softly, noticeably calmer than moments prior.

"We should get going now. We wouldn't want to waste any more time if we wanted to catch up to Ilana." Vulcan said, with a gentle sigh.

I nodded as Vulcan wrapped Gordon's arm around his shoulder to stabilize him. I followed them out of the guest room and further down the never-ending hallway to the large spiral staircase that would take us to the main floor.

As we traveled through the castle, I began to worry for Lala's mental stability, remembering the episode Gordon had gone through. I couldn't bear the thought of her suffering through one as well, her heart torn between hope and despair. More questions began to speculate within the depths of my mind before the sound of my brother's voice shattered my train of thought.

"Hey, you're doing that thing again," Vulcan said, now walking beside me.

"What thing?"

"Y'know, the thing. Where you space out and have this solemn look on your face. Come on, tell me what's up."

"Something's been bothering me for a while now," I started, then paused.

"Well duh. Spill. What's up?" Vulcan retorted, half-joking.

"How did the elves find us? I was almost positive we hadn't been followed, so how were they able to locate her? I doubt she told anyone she was leaving home, but they found us as soon as we got here. I have this feeling in my gut that something's off. I can't put my finger on why."

"Well, you got me there. I have no idea." Vulcan said contemplatively, his voice holding the same concern I felt within my soul.

"Actually, you're right. The fact that they found her makes no sense at all." Gordon chimed in.

"Is it possible they found her by chance?" Vulcan asked me as we turned another corner and walked down another hallway.

"I highly doubt it," I answered pensively, reminiscing about the distance Lala and I had traveled.

"Strange," Vulcan said deep in thought. "I come up empty. I have no idea."

"Maybe we should ask when we find them?" Gordon suggested.

"Yeah, I guess we kinda have to," I replied, at a loss for any other ideas.

"By the by, our destination is right outside these doors. I took us out of the back exit of the castle. This will take us through a secluded escape route so that we can leave here unnoticed." Vulcan shoved open the two large wooden doors that stood before us.

The blinding morning sun's rays poured through the open door, casting a brilliant illumination that bathed the corridor in a warm and radiant light. The golden hues danced along the walls, creating intricate patterns of light and shadow that seemed to breathe life into the once-dim passageway. The air felt fresh and invigorating, carrying with it a gentle breeze that rustled the curtains and carried the faint scent of blooming flowers. The soft chirping of birds outside provided a cheerful soundtrack to the scene, blending harmoniously with the gentle hum of activity within the castle walls. As I stood there, taking in the beauty of the moment, I couldn't help but feel a sense of renewal and hope wash over me, as if the world itself was waking up to greet a new day filled with endless possibilities. I blinked through the burning pain in my eyes to see the shadow-plagued path that weaved behind residential buildings within our castle walls. At first, I didn't recognize the surrounding area, but as we traveled further down the dusty stone path I stopped dead in my tracks.

"Merlin, what's wrong?" Vulcan asked.

"Th-this is where they took her away from me," I stammered in shock.

"How is that possible? Very few people know about this exit. It's an escape route for the royal family if things ever came down to something like that." Vulcan's brow furrowed with concern.

"Is it possible they could have walked around the wall and found it?" Gordon suggested in an attempt to calm our anxieties, but Vulcan shook his head.

"It's hidden by magic from the outside. Only someone with classified knowledge of the kingdom's structure and layout would know about this." Vulcan's face dropped, his features contorting into a disgruntled expression that mirrored his inner turmoil.

"Vulcan, what is it?" Gordon's brows furrowed as he looked at us with concern etched across his face. His eyes held a mixture of anxiety and curiosity as if he were bracing himself for an answer that he wasn't quite sure he wanted to hear. His lips parted slightly, ready to form words that would give voice to his worries. The subtle lines on his forehead deepened as he awaited our response, his posture tense and attentive. His hands fidgeted slightly, fingers tapping against his thigh in an unconscious rhythm. There was an unmistakable urgency in his gaze, a plea for reassurance or clarity that we might be able to provide. As the weight of his question hung in the air, it was clear that whatever had prompted it was weighing heavily on his mind, and he was searching for some semblance of solace amidst the uncertainty.

"There is no doubt about it," said Vulcan, face consumed by shadows.

Gordon and I both fixated our anxious gazes on him, our minds blank about what might be transpiring within his thoughts.

"Talon was involved in this," Vulcan whispered. His voice wavered slightly as he spoke. His eyes, usually so steadfast, now held a complex blend of hurt, anger, and a touch of betrayal. The weight of his realization was etched onto his features, causing his brow to furrow and his lips to tighten.

As the words hung in the air, the world seemed to grow still, the gravity of the situation sinking in for all of us. Vulcan's gaze remained fixed ahead as if trying to process the enormity of the act committed by someone who was supposed to be a trusted sibling. The bond that had once connected them now seemed strained, overshadowed by the actions that had fractured it.

I felt my own heart drop inside my chest as a gasp escaped my lips. A surge of shock paralyzed both my mind and body, leaving me unable to grasp the whirlwind of emotions that flooded over me at that moment. Our very own brother, in an act that cut deep, not only turned against our family and me but also betrayed our kingdom and the very people he was meant to protect and serve. I struggled to comprehend how he had become entangled in this situation. It felt like a nightmare that I desperately wished to awaken from. I felt cold and my body began to shake as a tsunami of anxiousness crashed into me.

"We need to find Lala if what you both are saying is right," Gordon said, pulling his arm from around Vulcan as he turned to face us. "Based on your expressions and energy, I can assume that his involvement can mean nothing good. It brings me great sorrow to say that I think I may know what's going on, and I think I may know who your brother is."

"What? How-?" I started but trailed off.

Without uttering another word, Vulcan bolted towards the exit, flinging the door wide open and dashing beyond the boundaries of the kingdom's grounds. Taken aback by his abrupt actions, Gordon and I exchanged glances before swiftly following in pursuit. My body felt like it was weighed down by the burden of malnutrition and dehydration, a result of the prolonged depressive episode I had been enduring. Despite the discomfort and pain, I pushed forward with a determination that overshadowed the physical sensations. I had to catch up to Vulcan before I would lose him too.

"Vulcan stop!" Gordon's voice echoed as we crossed the boundary of Camelot's territory.

I clenched my jaw as I used every last bit of energy I had to catch up to my brother and grab his arm tightly. He struggled and tried to pull away from me, but I did not allow it.

"Vulcan, we can't afford to lose our cool right now," I grunted as his thrashing body squirmed.

"Listen to me. Look into my eyes and take a deep breath," huffed Gordon as he threw his hands upon my brother's shoulders.

Vulcan's face softened as he obeyed Gordon's orders. For a split second, I thought I could see the shimmering of a single tear rolling down his face, but as I blinked it was gone. Witnessing Vulcan shed tears over something was so rare that it made me doubt the validity of what I thought I had observed.

"I apologize. I don't know what came over me." With a sigh, Vulcan uttered, weighed down by the heavy sorrow that enveloped him.

"Don't apologize for that. There is no need, lad." Gordon's words were laden with comfort as he spoke.

Vulcan nodded before he said, "Well, we made it regardless."

I glanced at him, my expression etched with confusion as his words left me puzzled. We found ourselves positioned in an open expanse behind the castle, surrounded by nothing but trees, while the dark outlines of mountains formed a backdrop in the distance. How could we possibly be at our destination?

"Excuse me?" I inquired, my confusion evident in my tone.

"Here watch this," He responded with a smirk, then closed his eyes and lifted his hand towards the sky.

An aerospace orange magic swirled up from his body to his hand, then burst upward towards the clouds. His eyes, ablaze with fiery orange, shot open and began to glow.

"Hear my call, Egan!" With confidence, Vulcan let out a resounding scream to the realm beyond the clouds.

Before I could fully comprehend the unfolding scene, a burst of vibrant orange light pierced the sky, casting an illuminating glow, and a colossal crimson dragon with an enigmatic figure astride emerged, descending toward us.

"Who or what is that?" Taken aback by the sudden turn of events, I asked with a startled tone.

"That, brother, is Prince Egan Ahearn– the humanoid draconic half-breed! He's an old friend of mine," Vulcan announced, dropping his arm before turning to grin at me.

I watched in awe as the enormous draconic beast slammed its monstrous claws into the grassy earth before its rider flamboyantly lept from its back to engage us in conversation.

"You summoned me, Vulcan?" Egan asked before pulling my brother into a tight embrace.

"It's been a while, Egan. How's the family?" Vulcan asked before respectfully pulling away.

"They have been well and my dragon, Helios, has been better than ever," he responded with a smile.

"That is wonderful to hear!" Vulcan's voice held a note of genuine happiness as he responded, his eyes lighting up with enthusiasm.

"Why is it that you summoned me to this realm?" Egan's voice was tinged with caution as he inquired, his demeanor wary and alert.

Vulcan's tone was urgent as he spoke, his words carrying a weight of concern. "We need your help. Merlin's elvish girlfriend, or whatever you want to call her, has been abducted by two of her own kind, and they've got their hands on some classified information," he explained, the gravity of the situation evident in his voice.

"She's not my-" I started before I was interrupted by Egan.

"I understand what you are asking of me. Helios and I would be honored to assist you, dear friend." He said with a kind smile.

Vulcan's voice held a mix of determination and gratitude as he spoke, his eyes focused on Egan. "I will repay both of you in any way necessary," he declared, the sincerity in his words underscoring his commitment to the cause.

"Hop onto my dragon's back and hold on tightly. I trust you to grab the reins, Vulcan," Egan said, his tone firm and confident as he gestured toward the waiting winged beast.

"Wait, but what about you?" I inquired as I assisted Gordon in getting onto the dragon's back.

"I'll be flying right beside you," Egan said with a playful wink as scarlet magic enveloped his back, expanding into two massive draconic wings.

"That's incredible!" Gordon exclaimed, admiring our unique new companion.

"Alright, let's get this show on the road," Vulcan declared, his grip firm on the hickory-colored leathery reins.

"Are you ready?" Gordon inquired, his arms encircling Vulcan, gesturing for me to do the same.

I nodded determinedly, my resolve firm. Everything led to these moments. My whole life, fate had paved this path before me to bring her to me. Above all else, I held her in the highest regard, cherishing her beyond measure, and I wasn't willing to let her slip away from my life indefinitely. A fierce determination took hold of me, and I made an unshakable vow to myself at that very moment. I was resolute that I would locate Lala, and I was committed to setting things right, regardless of the sacrifices it might demand. No matter what happens, I wouldn't rest until she was by my side once more. *Non Desistas Non Exieris*– Never give up, never surrender.

CHAPTER 8

Ad astra per aspera, "Through adversity to the stars" was a saying I grew quite fond of as a young child. I would always tell my brother, Reed, that I would overcome adversities to create my own fate and pave my own path toward the future. I wanted to believe that I was strong enough to change the world around me one step at a time. I longed for the strength to conquer the challenges that stood before me, yet now I find myself incapable of achieving even that. All I could do was helplessly watch as I was torn away from my beloved Merlin. I felt utterly powerless in the face of that situation, and the sense of helplessness disgusted me to my core.

"We're almost home. Just a few more miles to go, Freya," Gwen said sternly before frowning at my bleak expression.

"Ilana, are you just going to sit there and sulk? You've been sulking for days now," she asked me, her tone lacking true concern. Her words struck a chord, exposing the depth of my despondency.

I lacked the energy to reply. Moving felt like an insurmountable task, as I was burdened by a heavy numbness, a result of the pain I was carrying. I could only imagine the hell I put Merlin through and for that, I could never forgive myself. Through the static and emptiness, one clear question remained in my mind. How had they found me? I hadn't told anyone where I was going, nor did I leave a trail for them to follow me. Not that it mattered in the end, what happened was reality whether or not I wanted it to be. I had to try to move on…

Who was I kidding, I could never move on from this. The aftermath of this tragedy left irreparable damage in its wake. Even if I were to encounter him once more, I knew he would never grant me his forgiveness, and to be honest, I wouldn't anticipate it either. Lying is considered an unforgivable transgression for good reason. My actions were heartless, and no matter how many times I longed to rewind time and alter the past, I must accept that the deed is irrevocable. There was no way around that reality, and that was what pained me the most.

"H-how did you find me?" I asked, mustering the only remaining willpower I had.

"Some human guy tipped us off. Said he saw a young elvish girl and the youngest Camelot prince and told us where to find you," Gwen responded.

"This strange hooded mage that was with him showed us a secret entrance into the kingdom, though I'm not sure how he knew about it," Freya chimed in, reflecting on the individuals they had encountered during their journey to retrieve me.

My face wrinkled in confusion. I hadn't remembered running into anyone along the way except-

"What was his name?" I asked, my eyes widening in realization.

"Oh, I don't know. Albert or Alexander or something like that," Freya said.

"Alastor." A sinking feeling gripped my chest, and a wave of nausea began to wash over me.

"Yeah, that was his name. Eh, why do you ask?" Gwen's expression twisted with confusion as she sought to make sense of the situation.

Nausea churned within me, and I instinctively raised my bound hands to shield my mouth. Tears streamed down my face, engulfing me in sheer horror.

"Ilana, what's the matter?" Freya's voice carried a note of seriousness as she addressed me, her gaze fixed on my distressed state.

"Did he happen to see which direction you came from?" My words were tense, the urgency evident in my tone as I pressed for a response.

Freya's voice held a note of concern as she asked, "I don't know. Why are you so worried?" Her question cut through the tension, revealing her confusion about my sudden shift in behavior.

My urgency was palpable as I practically shouted, "Listen to me and listen carefully. We have to get back to the colony now." The words were forceful and laced with a sense of desperation, as I conveyed the gravity of the situation.

"Ilana, what's going on?" Gwen's voice trembled with the same fear I heard in Freya's tone as she inquired, her concern evident as she leaned over to release my previously bound hands.

With urgency and intensity, I explained, "You've been deceived. That man you conversed with is utterly wicked. He kidnapped and subjected both Merlin and me to torture. He's a heartless sociopath who will obliterate anything and everything in his pursuit of power." my voice carried a mix of anger and seriousness.

I sensed the shock of the predicament gradually sinking into their minds as they came to terms with the grave error they had committed. I couldn't fathom how, but Alastor managed to survive the explosions and harbored a thirst for revenge, and they unwittingly played right into his malevolent schemes. He was aware of their origins and poised to fulfill his desire—seizing power. I looked upward, peering through the gaps between leaves, only to have my fears confirmed by the thick columns of black smoke rising from my homeland.

"Damn it!" Gwen shouted in frustration and urged her horse to transition from a casual canter to a full-on gallop.

Freya and I followed as we hastily flew through the forest toward the blazing inferno that once was our peaceful colony. Behind us, a turbulent path of thorny brambles emerged, a result of the fusion of our druidic magic and the unbridled fury within us.

"I hope we aren't too late," Freya's voice trembled with fear, a soft whimper escaping her lips, as the flickering flames became visible through the thin veil of trees ahead.

"Me too, Freya. Let's just hope the damage is minimal," Gwen's voice held a firm tone as she concealed the pain that coursed through her.

Out of nowhere, a sphere of intense crimson magic materialized and hurtled straight toward us with alarming speed. The impact of the blast struck the ground just ahead of us, resulting in a powerful explosion that sent us and our horses hurtling backward.

In that fleeting moment, my body hung suspended in mid-air, surrounded by an eerie silence that seemed to stretch into infinity. Apart from my sight, all my other senses appeared to vanish, leaving me in a suspended state of sensory deprivation. I felt nothing, heard nothing, and smelled nothing. My thoughts appeared to dissolve into nothingness, and even my mind felt as if it had gone blank. Every moment seemed elongated, as if time itself had slowed down. I observed Gwen's unconscious face covered in soot and my sister's lifeless body, her form stained with blood, suspended beside me. In that fleeting moment, I perceived everything, but as quick as it happened, it had stopped, reality swiftly realigning. The throbbing pain in my head intensified, and a sharp, persistent ringing filled my ears, disorienting my senses.

I blinked my eyes open, greeted by a hazy and unfocused world as my vision struggled to regain clarity. Through my daze, I forced my achy body to sit up in an attempt to gather my bearings. I observed my surroundings, my vision blurring in and out of focus. The sight before me stirred a nauseating sensation in my stomach as I took it in. I spotted

Freya kneeling next to Gwen's charred form, her body marred with both blood and soot.

The grim scene included the shattered remains of what were once our horses a short distance behind them. I felt myself gag as I leaned over to expel anything that remained in my stomach. As I raised my head, Freya's mouth opened in what appeared to be a scream, though the explosion had left my ears ringing and the words were lost in the cacophony. My head was spinning and everything felt fuzzy, but I knew I couldn't just do nothing, so I forced my battered body to stand. I limped over to Freya who was now sobbing and at that moment I realized what she was trying to tell me. My childhood friend, my closest companion, was dead. Overwhelmed by my emotions, I grew lightheaded and let out a guttural scream of anguish that reverberated across the vast expanse around us. A tidal wave of black thorny vines surged forth from within me, fueled by an overwhelming rage, and enveloped a sizable area around both Freya and me. My common sense had betrayed me and wrath plagued my mind and body. I felt myself uncontrollably sprint towards the colony at a seemingly impossible speed and that's when I saw him, snickering at the damage he had dealt.

"Alastor, you bastard!" I screamed at the top of my lungs as I rushed towards him.

I felt a dark energy encompass my hand as I threw it forward, creating giant razor-sharp spikes that surged toward him. He evaded them with flamboyant movements, seemingly mocking my efforts, a sight that intensified the malice churning within my soul. All I consciously knew was that there and then I wanted to take his life.

"Ilana, don't!" I heard Freya's voice scream. "You can't come back from this if you kill him in the state you are in now."

It was too late. I found myself devoid of control over my actions, relentlessly thrusting spikes at his agile form.

"Oops, you missed me." Alaster tauntingly spoke, deliberately stoking my uncontrollable rage and thereby hindering my abilities from achieving their full potential through balance and concentration.

"Ilana stop this!" Freya yelled again, running towards me.

It was utterly futile as I was reduced to a hollow shell devoid of purpose or agency. As a last effort to halt me, Freya shut her eyes and initiated the sacred dance of the druids. Numerous thick basil-green vines burst forth from the earth and surged toward me, aiming to restrain me. My screams echoed as the vines wound tightly around my arms and legs, causing me to thrash about relentlessly.

"Aw, how sweet! You're doing my job for me!" Alastor cackled with a maniacal sneer as he conjured another ball of crimson magic. As the ball of magic hurtled towards me, my eyes widened and a rush of memories flashed through my mind.

I writhed against my constraints, desperate to live, but my efforts were fruitless.

"Ilana no!" Freya's desperate scream pierced the chaos, carrying a tone of helplessness and urgency that resonated through the turmoil around us.

I was immobilized, trapped in a timeless moment that seemed to stretch on in slow motion, as it had before. Just as I prepared myself for the premature caress of death's cold hands, a familiar blinding blue sphere of magic intercepted the crimson projectile, causing it to detonate a few feet away from me, burning through the vines that held my movements. I recognized the magical aura that radiated from the electric blue sphere. There was no doubt about it.

With my heart racing and tears welling up in my eyes, I shouted, "Merlin!" The overwhelming surge of joy and relief flooded through me.

"My apologies, m'lady. I didn't intend to arrive late to the party." He flashed a confident grin as he gracefully leaped from the back of the enormous winged beast, landing right beside me. "You aren't hurt are you?"

I smiled back at his enchanting demeanor and replied, "No, thanks to you."

"Three against one? Not fair!" Alastor yelled, enraged at his failed attack.

"Not quite!" Gordon yelled as he shot a glimmering green arrow of light at Alastor, grazing his shoulder.

"Y-you! When did you-" Alastor stammered as Gordon hopped to the ground beside Merin and me.

"Oh, and we brought some reinforcements!" Merlin said, pointing at Vulcan, Egan, and Helios who were still airborne.

"Nice to see you in one piece, princess," Vulcan yelled with a playful smile.

Tears welled up in my eyes as I took in the sight of my friends standing beside me, and I felt overwhelmed with emotion. Seeing Merlin and everyone else once again filled me with an overwhelming sense of relief.

"That's cheating!" Alastor let out a furious scream momentarily, but his olive green eyes then gleamed with a manic grin. "Luckily, I also brought some backup."

He whistled sharply, summoning a battalion of armored soldiers and a sizable goblin army led by cloaked spellcasters and mages.

"This should even the odds," Alastor bellowed as he flung yet another magical sphere toward Merlin, Gordon, and me.

"Look out!" Gordon shouted as he lunged at Merlin and me, forcing us to the ground to evade Alastor's attack.

"How the hell did he survive Gordon's explosives?" I asked Merlin, afraid and with my face displaying a mix of confusion and concern.

"I have no idea. It shouldn't be possible." Merlin replied, casting a quick glance at Gordon who nodded in agreement.

"Unlike my worthless pawns, I was able to shield myself with magic. As the explosives were detonated I protected myself, leaving me almost completely unscathed!" Alastor chuckled as he leisurely walked closer.

"You just let the others die?!" Gordon shouted, his anger fueled by Alastor's demeanor.

"What part of 'worthless pawns' do you not understand?" Alastor responded mockingly, further igniting the fury within Gordon.

"Don't let him get to you." Merlin said, "We need to get up before we get swarmed."

My voice trembled as I desperately exclaimed, "There are way too many of them! We can't possibly fight them all!"

"We'll have to, or we'll die trying." With confidence in his voice, Gordon propelled himself off the ground, slinging a flurry of arrows toward Alastor.

Amidst the chaos of the battle, Freya's urgent voice cut through the air as she threw thorn spears towards the encroaching enemy forces. "Ilana! Egan and I will cover you the best we can from here, but I don't think we'll be able to beat them all. What should we do?" Her words carried both concern and determination, highlighting the dire situation they found themselves in.

I clenched my teeth, quickly surveying the surroundings while Merlin sprang to his feet, dashing towards a group of spellcasters brandishing books, much like himself. I lacked an answer to Freya's inquiry. A sense of helplessness engulfed me, fueling my mind with a surge of anger. We were outnumbered. My introspection was suddenly ceased by wine-colored spheres of blazing magical energy flying straight toward me. I narrowly evaded their attacks, emerging unharmed. With my arms poised, I prepared to launch thorny vines at the cloaked mage who had targeted me. A grin formed on my lips as the thorny vines slammed the mage against a massive tree, rendering him unconscious.

"Freya, I don't know how to answer your questions. However, I do know that we need to keep fighting no matter what. We must protect the Great Willow Tree!" I said, glancing over to our sacred monument.

"Fools, you just gave away your biggest secret! Now I know what your druid treasure is!" Alastor cackled.

"Hey! Never take your eyes off your opponent!" Gordon shouted as he drew back an arrow.

Rage glinted in his eyes as he released his arrow, causing Alastor's eyes to widen before he hurled himself backward. The arrow grazed Alastor's side and his grin quickly turned into an angry scowl as he winced in pain.

"I'm getting quite annoyed with you. Now die!" Alastor screamed as both of his hands were engulfed by his crimson magic.

Without hesitation, Alastor hurled two massive energy spheres directly at Gordon. Gordon leaped backward in an attempt to evade them, but his efforts were in vain. Avoiding the first sphere, he collided with the smaller second one, sending him hurtling back like a ragdoll.

"Gordon!" With a scream, Vulcan rose on Helios's back and hurled fireballs at Alastor.

Tears streamed down my face, and a deep sense of despair overtook me as I watched the scene unfold. Anger and frustration surged through my thoughts once again. With a fierce glare fixed on Alastor, who effortlessly evaded Vulcan's onslaught, I dashed towards him, my scream of anger echoing in the air. I pulled my arm back, launching a spiky ball of thorns at him.

"Aw, how cute!" Alastor cackled as he charged at me as well.

"Lala, get out of there!" Merlin yelled, attempting to run towards me only to be stopped by the mysterious spellcaster that stood before him.

I disregarded Merlin and pressed on, charging towards Alastor. Once again, I drew my arm back, shaping a lightweight rapier crafted entirely from razor-sharp thorns. I didn't have time to indulge in shock from the new ability mid-battle. Alastor chuckled when he noticed my blade, mimicking my actions to conjure a heavier blade of crimson darkness. I shouted as our swords clashed with lightning speed, driving my blade against his with every ounce of strength I could muster.

"How dare you hurt my friend!" I screamed as I repeatedly slashed at him.

He chuckled as he persisted in parrying my strikes and remarked, "He was quite irritating. He got in my way."

"Is that all he was to you?! A worthless pawn?!" I shouted with growing fury, each blow driven by my mounting anger.

"Precisely," He laughed maniacally while casting a glance at Merlin, who was busy neutralizing the spellcasters with his electric blue spheres.

Before I could process what was happening, Alastor swiftly launched a small crimson needle at Merlin's torso, hitting him directly. In pain, Merlin let out a yelp and winced, leaving himself vulnerable to an attack. With horror, I witnessed the spellcaster's violet ball of magic knocking Merlin off his feet and onto the ground with a resounding thud. Vulcan swiftly descended on Helios's back to address the growing number of mages and spellcasters, taking his brother's place. All I could do was stare in terror as distress overwhelmed my thoughts.

"And now you're open!" Alastor's sudden scream snapped my attention back to him as I realized the danger he posed.

A surge of intense, sharp pain radiated from my back, causing my eyes to widen in shock. As I fell forward to the ground, I could feel a warm liquid trickling down my body. My mind was too consumed by shock to fully grasp what had happened. As my body lay on the tilted ground, I watched the surroundings blur while a tight hand wrapped around my throat. Facing Alastor, my body hung motionless above the ground in his grip.

"As fun as this was, I have work to do. Au revoir, Elven Princess Ilana." Alastor declared, raising a silver dagger from his belt and aiming it at my chest.

"I-I won't..." I huffed weakly, "I won't let you win... Alastor."

A deafening silence enveloped me as I could only watch in helplessness. Alastor's eyes glimmered with insanity as he drew his arm back, preparing to plunge his blade deep into my chest. A vivid memory seized control of my thoughts, flooding my mind with its detailed imagery. In my mind's eye, I saw my brother's face vividly, his eyes filled with determination as he fervently advised me to never lose hope. Summoning my last reserves of energy, I forcefully drove my foot into Alastor's lower abdomen, propelling myself away from him even as the blade penetrated my body. I threw myself backward, contorting my body into a ball as I executed a backflip to regain my footing. I pulled his dagger from its flesh-made sheath and swiftly tossed it to the ground.

"I will never let someone like you win!" I screamed as I stumbled backward, struggling to maintain my balance due to blood loss.

"Uragh. You stubborn pest! No matter, I'll just kill you now!" Alastor shouted enraged by my efforts to survive.

Out of nowhere, a sphere of vibrant chartreuse magic slammed into Alastor's chest, sending his body hurtling backward. The magic's energy was familiar, yet my mind couldn't quite comprehend it. I turned around with weakness, only to find my brother, Reed, glaring resolutely at the struggling Alastor, who was trying to stand up again.

"That's enough, Outsider." Reed's voice boomed aggressively. "First you burn down our colony, and now you try to kill my dear younger sister. You disgust me!"

"Who the hell are you?" Alastor's voice broke through the chaos as he looked at Reed with a mixture of confusion and frustration.

"I am your worst nightmare," Reed responded as he dashed towards Alastor at an unimaginable speed.

I gazed in wide-eyed astonishment at Reed's extraordinary abilities. I was rendered utterly speechless by the unfolding scene before me. His movements were faster than anything I had witnessed before. Even Alastor appeared bewildered by my brother's agility, evident from the sweat glistening on his forehead. Reed delivered a series of rapid punches toward Alastor, leaving him with no choice but to evade each one.

"How dare you harm these wonderful people! How dare you destroy my home! How dare you call yourself a human! You're nothing but a disgusting monster!" Reed screamed as one of his punches made contact with Alastor's face, knocking him off his feet once more.

A cry of agony escaped Alastor's lips as his body collided with the ground. His face which was once consumed by madness was now tainted with rage.

"You bastard! You're ruining everything!" Alastor's scream reverberated through the air as he pounded his crimson fists into the ground before him, causing the earth to tremble beneath Reed's feet. Reed stumbled backward before leaping into the air and landing back beside me.

"Ilana, can you fight?" Reed asked as he gazed into my azure eyes.

"Yes, I can," I responded, regaining full control of my body.

"Good. Let's finish this druid style," said Reed as he winked at me before gently grasping my hands.

With a resolute nod, I understood his intention. It was time for me to do something I had never been able to do before. The time had come for me to execute the Druid's Dance with him as my partner, aiming for a successful outcome. My eyes gleamed with unwavering determination as I met my brother's gaze. This was it. I had to do this. I sensed the storm of emotions within me settling down, replaced by a serene stream of energy flowing through my mind, body, and soul. I sensed myself moving gracefully in harmony with the energy surrounding me, my own energy intertwining seamlessly with Reed's. It was at that moment that there was only one dancer. My brother and I were perfectly synchronized with each other and the energy of the world around us. Alastor gritted his teeth as he began frantically throwing crimson spheres at us which we gracefully dodged as we continued our performance.

"No! Stay away!" Alastor's desperate screams echoed through the air as we gracefully moved around him, our combined energy forming a protective barrier. His frantic cries filled the atmosphere, a futile attempt to ward us off.

His body began to stiffen and solidify as our movements continued. The ground beneath his feet started creeping up his legs, triggering a mixture of struggle and panic within Alastor. Yet, neither my brother nor I paid heed to his distress, fully absorbed in our synchronized dance. With each fluid movement that Reed and I executed, my fear and pain began to fade, even as Alastor's enraged screams echoed through the forest. At the culmination of our dance, Alastor's wrath was quelled, replaced by the realization of his defeat, and his body and soul were encased by solid stone.

I hugged my brother tenderly, tears flowing freely down my cheeks. It was finally over. Leaving my brother's embrace, a numbness washed over me, and my body weakened as the pull of gravity took hold of my limbs. Before my lifeless form could descend to the ground, Reed dropped to his knees, cradling my wounded and battered vessel in his arms.

"You did a good job, Ilana. I'm so proud of you." He said as tears welled up in his chartreuse eyes.

My vision began to blur once again, the severity of my wounds taking its toll on my senses. As my eyelids began to droop, I could just barely discern another figure leaning over me. The individual standing beside Reed turned out to be none other than Merlin. He was alive! Through the haze of emotions that flowed through my half-conscious mind, I felt the warmth of contentment ease my soul. I faintly heard Merlin's voice inaudibly say something before the darkness of unconsciousness released me from reality's grasp.

CHAPTER 9

The sound of the explosions of magic and the ringing that pierced my deafened ears were the only sounds that consumed the atmosphere around me. I could faintly hear the grumbles of a voice, but I couldn't quite make out who they belonged to. As my senses came back to me I saw my brother, Vulcan, standing in front of me. He was fighting off a strange spellcaster in order to protect my fallen body.

"You're awake, that's good. Hurry up and give me a hand with this tough son of a bitch." Vulcan said half-jokingly as sweat rolled down his face.

"Right!" I said as I slowly crawled to my feet the pain rolled over my body like a steamroller, causing me to grunt.

"You have to push through it. Lala needs us. That jackass hurt her pretty badly," Vulcan said as he hurled a fireball at the spellcaster who as a result dodged it quickly in retaliation.

I gritted my teeth as I aggressively threw a ball of blue lightning at our foe, making contact with nothing but the charcoal gray hood that hid his face. His now-revealed snow-white hair glistened in the sunlight as he wore a shocked expression on his face. My eyes widened as I examined his familiar slender figure alongside his pale skin and that's when I realized who we had been facing. I'd recognize his ruby-red eyes anywhere. It was none other than my brother, Talon! He clenched his jaw and frantically pulled his tattered hood back over his eyes as he swiftly spun around to flee.

"T-Talon, wait!" I screamed as I started after him, reaching my hand out towards him.

I felt a sharp pain in my side where a long solidified crimson needle was, buried deep within me. I winced in pain and keeled over, scraping my knees on the ground.

"Damn it!" Vulcan screamed as he ran over to me to assist me back to my feet.

"We'll search for him later. We need to" I started before I felt a warm thick substance force itself from my throat.

I quickly drew my hand up to my mouth as I coughed up a red liquid. My eyes widened as I realized that it was blood. Fear settled in my mind as I began to panic. I knew that if I were coughing blood then my injuries were worse than I'd thought.

"Merlin! Tsk, this isn't good. We need a healer immediately," Vulcan said as he squatted, urging me to jump onto his back so as not to over-exert myself.

Though I was unhappy about taking help from my older brother, I accepted it with a grain of salt considering that I needed to survive. I wasn't about to allow myself to die, especially not now after everything that I had been through.

"Woah. Merlin, look over there." Vulcan said, nodding forward to guide me.

As I quickly scanned the area, my eyes fell upon Lala and an unfamiliar young elven male. The two elves were gracefully dancing around Alastor, who was screaming furiously at the top of his lungs. The way Lala and her dance partner were moving was enchanting, and the invisible magical veil that surrounded them filled my soul with a strange sense of tranquility.

"So this is the power of the druid wood elves? It's truly incredible!" Vulcan said in amazement.

"She did it. She finally unlocked her full potential." I said, allowing a stray tear of joy to roll down my cheek.

At that, their ballet concluded and the man that plagued this land was gone and frozen in stone. I was dumbfounded by what I had witnessed. I never would have guessed that Lala possessed this kind of power within her all this time. My eyes widened as her brutally beaten body collapsed into the stranger's cradling arms and I leaped from Vulcan's back to hobble over to them.

"Will she be okay?" I asked as I approached the young elvish man.

"I am not sure. She is in critical condition. We need to get her to the healing pools that lie beneath the weeping tree; our Great Willow Tree," he answered hastily.

I offered him my hand to assist him to his feet while holding onto Lala, but he scowled and ignored it. I was confused by his hostile behavior as I hadn't done anything to insult him. Not to mention I aided his colony in the fight against Alastor.

"What gives? Why are you being so cold towards me?" I dared ask.

"Your kind isn't usually welcome around these parts. Pardon my behavior, I have little trust for humanfolk." He responded, sincerely.

"Please, just allow me to help. She means everything to me. I can explain everything once we save her." I said, and I stumbled, only to be steadied by Vulcan's grasp.

"Fine, but you must do everything I say, exactly as I say it. Do you understand me?" He said before blowing a strand of his Arabian-green hair out of his face.

I nodded as he urged us to follow him toward a gigantic weeping willow tree. I glanced over to the left of us, and I saw Freya, who was carrying Gordon in her arms, and Egan, who had gently nudged Helios to stay put, following us with urgency.

"Will Gordon be alright?" I asked as I noticed his tattered body that was smeared in his dark mulberry blood.

"I hope so…" Freya said, her gaze drifting down in sorrow and she trailed off.

I sighed worriedly and returned my gaze to the massive tree that was before me. Its beautiful sage-green strings of leaves danced in the gentle breeze that wrapped itself around us. The dream-like atmosphere made me question what was real and what wasn't. It was all so miraculous. I shook my head to snap myself out of my trance-like daze, reminding myself of the obstacle that was at hand.

She may have defeated our opponent, but Lala couldn't be done fighting. Not yet. I would stay there, at her side, until she won, and her beautiful blue eyes opened once more.

"Aperta!" Reed yelled, flinging his arms toward the direction of the Great Willow Tree.

Unbelievably, before my very eyes, the tree's giant roots unraveled themselves, pulling open and revealing the entrance to a small descending spiral staircase. Reed started down them, and I hobbled after him in awe. I had never seen such powerful spellcasting before. I once more glanced over at Gordon's body, concernedly. His injuries looked severe based on the deep color of his blood.

"We need to cover Gordon's wounds, otherwise he will bleed out!" I shouted frantically, as I began to turn towards Freya.

"No! There is no time, hurry!" Reed yelled, before breaking out into a sprint down the staircase within the tree.

As I grit my teeth through the pain, I sprint after Reed, urging Freya and Egan to do the same. We hurriedly followed Reed into the sacred tree and began to stumble down the stairway. The thick-rooted steps felt firm beneath my feet as I descended into the unknown. With each step downward, my field of vision decreased until suddenly I realized that I was blinded by the absence of light. However, just as I went to speak up, a bright cerulean light illuminated the staircase before us. As the light brightened, the stairs flattened into the ground, and before us was a large dome-shaped chamber, outlined by effulgent cerulean orbs of magical light. Along the walls of the chamber were thirteen large circular pools of azure water-like liquid. My eyes sparkled with wonder as they darted around the room we had entered. My focus drifted to the dozens of elvish civilians gathered fearfully in the back wall of the alcove.

"Ilana!" shouted a loud unfamiliar voice which was full of panic and desperation.

I turned to see Reed slowly lowering Ilana's body into one of the healing pools, and a young man, looking to be around a similar age as Reed, sprinting over to aid him.

"Is she…?" he started, but his voice trailed off grimly.

"No, not yet at least. Hurry and start the incantation!" Reed said, frantically.

The young man nodded and started muttering something I couldn't quite make out under his breath. His eyes began glowing white and, to my surprise, a sphere within his chest began to glow as well. I glanced over to a healing pool further within the alcove, spotting Freya and another young elvish woman performing the same ritual on Gordon. I watched in astonishment as Lala's body began to sink beneath the surface of the water.

A sudden hand on my shoulder caused me to jump and whip my body around to face its beholder.

"Shhh! Come with me. We mustn't disrupt them." cooed the voice of an elder elvish woman, as she pushed her soft white hair from her wrinkled face.

I nodded and followed her toward the rest of the timid elvish colony.

"What is your name, human boy? Why are you here?" the woman softly asked.

"My name is Merlin, and I am the prince of a human kingdom called Camelot." I responded, "I'm friends with Lala- I mean Princess Ilana."

"I see…" She trailed off.

"Have I done something wrong?" I asked nervously.

"Not at all, my child." She replied, gently.

My gaze fell to my feet, as my body tensed in fear of insulting the woman. I didn't know what to say, or what I was to do. I felt anxious and awkward, but then I remembered Lala's soft gentle smile and I felt a growing strength within my chest.

I might not be able to help with anyone's injuries, but there is one wound I had the power to help heal.

I smiled and said, "I wish to mend the damage caused by those before me, and form an alliance between our kingdoms."

Several audible gasps escaped the mouths of those who were listening. I watched as the woman looked down for a long while, appearing to be deep within her thoughts. She suddenly looked up, directly into my eyes.

"If what you say is true," she said gently, though her expression betrayed a firm solemnity, "then I must ask a few questions of you."

"I will answer to the best of my ability," I replied, handing over my heart as I bowed my head to her.

She watched me sternly as she asked, "What is it that drives you?"

"I wish to protect those I cherish."

She nodded, slow, in acceptance of my answer. She gave no indication if it was what she was looking for, instead moving on to, "There are three items in front of you; a rock, a feather, and a looking glass. Which do you choose, and why?"

"The... feather. I have always felt a connection to the wind, and the feather can enjoy it as I do."

"Very peculiar..." she said, though I had no way of knowing how, or why. "You see someone mugging a stranger from another race, how would you react?"

"I would attempt to reason with the aggressor, try to bargain for a peaceful resolution, then ensure the wellbeing of the victim."

Her stony countenance cracked, just a bit, as she raised an eyebrow. "If there is no such resolution?"

"I would defend the innocent. If there is no recourse but to fight, I will, but it is not something I wish to do needlessly."

"A noble response," she said, her expression returning to unreadable stone. "I ask of you now to describe yourself with an animal."

I paused as I lost myself in my thoughts. I hadn't ever thought of an animal to describe myself before, and, at such an important moment, none I could think of felt right. As time ticked ever forward, the crowd around us began to murmur.

Suddenly, a hazy memory from my childhood reared its head. It brought with it a comforting feeling of soft warmth, and I felt a serene smile creep across my face. When I was young, my mother and I would admire the sparrows that fluttered around the gardens, listening to their songs and watching them dance in the wind.

"A sparrow," I said softly, then raised my voice and my head. "I would choose a sparrow to describe myself."

She went quiet for a moment, staring at me, a hand resting over her lips as if she were considering something. Then she took my hands in hers. They were thin, bony with age, and cold.

"This is my final question," she said, and she looked me in the eye. She was serious, which was etched onto her face and cut out from her eyes. "Solemnly do you swear to treat the needs of my people with equal import to the needs of your own?"

"I do," I said. It was no loud declaration, but it had rung deep in my chest just the same.

"You have a kind soul and a heart as pure as the finest gold," the woman said, patting my left hand as she cradled it. "Are you sure you are ready to bear such a burden?" asked the woman, sternly.

Without hesitation or a second thought, I nodded, clenching my fist in determination. The silence around us quickly filled with whispers and murmurs. I felt the stares of the elves around me, but it didn't bother me. I knew that this was what Lala wanted and that thought fueled my soul with conviction.

"So, you wish to ally with us?" a familiar masculine voice called out from behind me.

I quickly turned around to see Reed and the other elvish male standing before me.

"Yes, indeed I do," I responded strongly.

"How do we know we can trust you? I mean, you are a human after all," Reed said agitatedly.

"Brother Reed, the village elder gave him her blessing. Who are we to argue?" the young man said, gently.

"I am Reed, the heir to the throne, I am the one who is in charge here-" Reed started before the other boy cut him off.

"But is that what father would have wanted? A tyrant of a ruler?"

Reed's chartreuse eyes widened before he looked down shamefully.

"I wish no harm upon the elves," I said calmly, "I wish to protect the people Ilana holds dearest to her."

"Calem is right. My father would have never wanted a tyrannical ruler, and if mother were here, she would disapprove of my actions. If the elder finds you worthy of a treaty with us, then I shall allow it," Reed said bitterly before storming off.

"Don't mind my brother. He has distrust for many races, including the humans," Calem said kindly as he pushed a loose lock of hair back into place behind his ear.

"I see. I don't blame him, especially not after all of this." I said, wistfully.

"He'll come around, just give him some time," Calem reassured me, as his canary yellow eyes pierced mine.

I nodded at him before walking back towards the pool that safeguarded Lala. I desperately craved her gentle voice to once again enchant my ears. As I looked at her, so frail and asleep, I found that her wounds had disappeared, healed over as if they hadn't happened at all.

"Amazing isn't it?" Vulcan's voice rang out from beside me.

"I have no words…" I said in awe.

"That's the elvish race for ya." chuckled Vulcan lightly.

"It's incred-" I started, but the sudden glowing of mint green light captivated my attention.

And then, miraculously, Lala's body rose above the water, suspended in the air and surrounded by a mint green luminescence. I was in awe of the magic around me. Bright swirling lights wrapped themselves around Lala, then danced free, spinning and spinning and spinning around the room, filling my vision with light.

And then she woke up.

Before I could react, she threw her body into me causing me to lose my balance and collapse backward with her tightly cradled in my arms. "Lala," I breathed, awe on my tongue as she squeezed her face against my shoulder.

When she pulled back, just enough to look up at me, her gaze captivated me.

Here she was, in my arms, well and awake.

I left no room for second-guessing and pressed my lips onto hers, soft as satin and gentle as a spring breeze. I felt a soft breath of surprise tickle against my skin before she moved a hand to my face.

I felt impossibly warm as she cradled my cheek and leaned into me.

I wished the moment would never end, but my lungs burned, and I pulled away. As I looked at her face, her cheeks were flushed and her eyes were still closed. When she blinked them open, slowly, they were dark, dilated. She smiled, rubbing her thumb against my cheek.

"I love you," she whispered, snatching the words from my lips. "I love you, Merlin."

My heart burned with joy, and I pulled her back into my embrace. "Lala, I love you too. I love you, and never again watch you be taken away. I never should have."

She laughed against my shoulder, squeezing me in return.

"Finally," Vulcan called a laugh in his voice, "you two admit it to each other. Took ya long enough."

I rolled my eyes and gently assisted Lala to her feet, but even then, I did not let her go. She squeezed my hand and didn't either.

"How is Gordon? Is he alive?" Lala asked, trying desperately to hold onto hope.

"He will be alright, thanks to our people," Calem said, stepping into sight with a joyous gleam in his eyes.

"Calem!" Lala launched for her brother, her hand slipping from mine.

"You had us worried, Ilana," Reed said, standing at his siblings' side and patting Lala's head.

"I know, and I'm deeply apologetic for my actions. I just-" Lala started before she was cut off by Reed.

"Shhh," he soothed. "It's okay. You're back now. You're safe."

Something seemed wrong to Lala, though, even as tears began to bud in her eyes. "Reed," she said, her brow furrowing and her voice wavering. "Why isn't Father here to scold me?"

Reed's expression faltered from the carefully composed calm, and tears welled within his own eyes. They slipped, unfettered, down his cheeks. "Lala…"

Lala's breath stuttered, and she shook her head. "No," she whispered, her voice trembling. "Where is he? Why isn't he—"

"It's not your fault," Calem interrupted, though he was no less composed, his voice thick with emotion. "Lala… Ilana…"

"If I hadn't left—"

"He wouldn't want you blaming yourself," Reed said, his voice breaking as he rubbed the tears away from his face. "None of us do. It isn't your fault, Ilana. It never was."

Her knees gave way as the truth hit her all at once, her mind refusing to grasp the words, yet her heart already knew. She choked on a sob, barely managing to get the words out. "Father… he's…?"

Reed nodded, unable to speak, while Calem gently held her shoulders, guiding her to the floor as her legs buckled beneath her. The weight of grief crashed over her, suffocating.

Her brothers both pulled her into a hug, their warmth doing little to ward off the cold that had settled in her chest. "I'm so glad you're back," one of them whispered, though the words were a blur in her ears.

Despite my best efforts to be happy that Lala was getting the comfort she needed, I couldn't quash the pang of sorrow that stung in my chest as I remembered the last sight of my own eldest brother. That frightened look in his eyes, then him running away.

A sudden hand on my shoulder caused me to wince as a familiar voice spoke, "We will get him back in time. Today, rejoice, for we stand victorious" Vulcan rubbed my back gently, trying to ease my mind.

"Yes, that is true… but for how long?" Lala spoke, pulling away from her brothers.

"Does anyone know who that was and why he attacked us?" Calem asked.

"He was an evil man who went by the name Alastor," I said, shivering at the memory of what he had done. "I'm not sure why he attacked your colony."

"I think I may know why," a weak voice called out.

I whipped around to see Gordon stumbling towards us with Freya's assistance. He looked almost as good as new, though he limped and leaned heavily on Freya's shoulder. I was relieved to see him alive after enduring a direct hit from Alastor's magic.

"Gordon!" Lala exclaimed, turning towards him. "You're okay!" She rushed to him, wrapping her arms around him.

"It's gonna take more than that to keep me down and out." Gordon chuckled faintly, patting Lala's head. He coughed, and Lala pulled away, concern painted on her face.

"Easy does it now," Vulcan said softly as he approached Gordon. "Here, I have you now." He scooped Gordon into his arms and carried him over to our group.

Lala followed at Vulcan's side, and Gordon tried to hide his face, burning bright red.

"I would like to hear what you know," Reed said. "We have lived here in peace for generations. If you know why we were suddenly targeted, we need that information."

Gordon shook his head, doubtless trying to ease some of his embarrassment even as Vulcan still held him. Vulcan said gingerly as he swiftly scooped up Gordon in his arms and carried him over to us.

I could see Gordon blush slightly before trying to hide his expression behind a veil of his Waitrose-green hair. I smiled a little and chuckled before refocusing my attention on the problem at hand.

"We've lived a peaceful life for many decades, it is hard for me to believe that this was an isolated incident," Reed said grimly.

"Regrettably, I have to agree with you." Gordon concurred.

"What do you mean?" I asked puzzledly.

"I overheard something a while ago," he said, patting Vulcan's arm as he finally let him stand on his own feet, "when I was working under Alastor about some plan to become supreme emperor, but I don't think he was talking about himself." Gordon started, trailing off deep into thought.

Confused, I asked, "I thought he wanted power?"

"Yes, Alastor was power-hungry, but he had no interest in leadership. I think he was working for someone. I don't know who." Gordon leaned into Vulcan's shoulder, biting at his thumb.

"That doesn't sound good at all," said Calem, his brow furrowed.

"If that's true, we could be looking at a full-scale war in our future," Reed concluded, crossing his arms.

"War?" Lala squeaked. "Now hold on, aren't we being a little hasty here?"

"I'm afraid not, lass."

"If it's war, Vulcan or I at least need to return to Camelot. We cannot help in any official capacity without a declaration signed by the king."

"That won't be easy considering what happened the last time," said Vulcan.

"Well, we need to try! We can't just sit here and do nothing! This could be the whole world that's at risk!" I said as I felt rage start to boil deep within me.

"Merlin, even if we did get our parents on board with this, it wouldn't be enough to hold off an entire army! We don't even know how many soldiers and fighters there are, nor do we know what their strength and skill levels are," Vulcan shouted.

"I could try to get my colony to join your forces, Prince Reed. Wood elves must stick together," said Gordon, trying to calm the dangerous waves of aggression that raged between my brother and me.

"More allies would be optimal for these circumstances," Reed responded practically.

"That settles it," I said, trying to sound official. "Gordon, Lala, and I will head to Camelot and then the northern elf colony."

I saw the shocked look on Lala's beautiful face and took a deep breath. I had volunteered her to leave her home when she had only just returned, out of my own selfish desire to keep her close, to always know she was safe and well, to personally ensure it.

"Merlin, everything will be alright," Lala said, placing her soft, smooth hand against my cheek and jolting me out of my own head. "Trust me."

"A world of war and fighting is not a world I want to see and a world I do not wish for you to reside in," I spoke softly, trying to mask my fear.

"Nor I, but we have to accept what's happening even if we don't wish to.".

"War brings great loss and sorrow, it's a form of violence that no one wishes upon. It's something that can change lives for the worse, especially when you lose someone you love," said Gordon attentively.

Everything fell silent as if we all had something to say but couldn't be heard behind the mirrors that masked our fear. I could tell that Lala was on edge, but I didn't know what to say or do to ease her troubles, for I was feeling the same anguish and fear. I had read about war in scrolls within the archives of Camelot and remembered the loss and destruction that came with it. No amount of texts or books would be enough to prepare us for what we feared would come. I shook my head, bringing me back to the world in front of me, but I still couldn't figure out what to say to ease the tension that resonated within us. My brother's voice finally broke the silence, freeing us from our soundproof graves.

Vulcan broke the silence. "Egan, Helios, Gordon, and I will return to our homelands. Merlin, stay with Lala here. She needs you right now, and her people need her here. See how you can help out around here." He turned to Reed and bowed his head. "Thank you for your generosity and hospitality. We will return once we've fulfilled our obligations to this peace agreement."

"We will see each other again very soon," Gordon said, offering a smile, "that is a promise. Be safe." Gordon said with a smile.

Without another word, Vulcan picked Gordon up once again, then turned and walked away. *Amor et melle et felle est fecundissimus*– Love is rich with both honey and venom.

CHAPTER 10

Alea iacta est. "The die has been cast." Our elvish soldiers knew this well and understood. I too was becoming familiar with this phrase, as bloodshed and violence draped its icy hand over our once peaceful sky. There was no way to escape what was to come, all we could do was accept it and prepare to the best of our ability. My colony began to bud from beneath the layer of ash that battle had left in its wake, and I hoped that, with time, it would come to bloom stronger than before. Each day, more and more structures were restored, and my people were hard at work to rebuild our homes. Though our colony grew stronger with each cycle of the moon, the loss of our king left us vulnerable and feeble. Alastor's incursion led to much dismay and discord, but it also reminded us of the terrible cruelties that existed in life. With my father deceased and my mother missing, my brother Reed was next to claim the throne and the responsibility for our people's fate. My heart ached remembering the times before I met Merlin when my family was once whole, but I would shake away the thoughts of the past reminding myself the only path is ahead of me, not behind.

"Lala, it's time to go," a familiar gentle voice called out, "are you ready?"

"Indeed I am, Merlin," I responded softly as I gently placed my pen back in its original place on my desk and rose from my cushioned chair.

I began to walk to my door before turning to face my oval-shaped silver mirror that rested vertically on my pastel green wall. My Swedish blonde hair was loosely pulled into a bun, with a fancy braid wrapped around it. I gently brushed a loose strand of hair behind my ear before gently running my hand along the lace of my elegant early spring green gown. Small pastel pink, yellow, baby blue and white flowers danced around the lace in a beautiful pattern, and gentle lace ribbon sleeveless straps held up the chic sweetheart neckline of my dress. With one last soft tug of the lace ribbon that wrapped itself around me, above my waist, the admiration of my appearance ended, and I continued towards the entrance of my bedroom.

"Wow, you look... *beautiful*," Merlin said in awe of my royal elvish apparel before he fidgeted with his unnaturally slicked-back hair.

Before responding I glanced at his Victorian aristocratic blue and black patterned vest that rested over his button-up midnight black dress shirt. My gaze shifted to his tight black dress pants held firmly to his waist by a slick black belt and then down to the black loafers that encased his feet.

"You look rather opulent and handsome yourself," I smiled, admiring him.

"It feels a bit… awkward," Merlin giggled, noticing that I wasn't accustomed to seeing him in such a manner. "I look strange, don't I?"

I laughed along with him, "Yeah, it is very different from the Merlin I'm used to."

We both joked for a few more moments before collecting ourselves. Merlin lightly grasped my hand as we began to make our way to the Great Willow Tree where Reed's coronation would be. Memories of that family meal the night before my departure from my colony flashed into my mind as we exited the building that used to be my home. I blinked back fragile tears as I remembered life always moving forward, never back.

As we continued walking towards the tree, I felt the eyes of my people fall upon us as we walked past and a sea of whispers followed. Many people in my colony had never seen a human before, and a relationship outside our race was unheard of. Many elves were encouraging and accepting of my relationship with Merlin, but others openly opposed it. I felt nervous and unnerved by the murmurs and glances shared around me. I struggled to keep my noble posture as I began to feel self-conscious and insecure. The stare of hundreds of pairs of eyes burned into me, and my skin itched. They were watching me, scrutinizing my every movement, every minute change in my face, my gait, looking for something, anything, perhaps even nothing, they could use to condemn me. My heart raced, throbbing loudly in my ears and clogging my throat. I was being measured, and my people may just find me lacking.

In the midst of the turmoil, I longed for the freedom to escape from this relentless scrutiny, to reclaim the quiet corners of myself where I could simply be without the weight of their collective gaze bearing down upon me. Merlin appeared to have noticed this, as he raised my hand to his lips and softly kissed it before tightening his grip as we took our traditional seats upon the weeping willow's roots beside my family and our close friends.

I stared into the crowd of elves gathered before us, and I felt my heart sink in sorrow, knowing our population was smaller than before. I quickly pushed my intrusive thoughts into the back of my mind as Reed and our colony's elder, Laurel, emerged from the tree's hidden cove, and stood before us. Within seconds it became eerily quiet, even the forest seemed to devote itself entirely to the coronation.

"For many moons, our colony had kept to itself in order to maintain the balance between peace and brutality." Laurel's voice echoed around our village and the surrounding forest, and she looked forward steadily as she spoke. "However, evil always finds a way to disrupt the tranquility of life. Our quiescence led to our weakness that revealed itself weeks ago; ill-preparedness when evil came knocking. That being said, let this coronation be an oath instead of a swan song filled with empty promises. Let this new era bring us hope and strength instead of pain and torment. Our beloved king is dead, but he is not gone. He lives and breathes within our hearts, and within the soul of his eldest son, brought before you today."

Cheers and yells of determination could be heard stirring up amongst the crowd as our elder spoke. Even I felt the sparks of her words ignite the fire that lay dormant within my heart. Each phrase carried a weight of wisdom, and the resonance of her voice seemed to weave a tapestry of inspiration around my soul. The fire that had slumbered within me was now fanned to life, its flames dancing with newfound purpose and guiding me out of the shadows of uncertainty. The wisdom in her words soothed the restless energy within me, focusing it on the wellbeing of my colony and my family, rather than the frustrating anxiety it had been. My eyes grew firm with conviction and fortitude as a smile spread across my face. At that moment, I realized the change in me since the day I met Merlin. It rang loud like the bells of a great choir before the holy church. Before my mind could match my emotions, my body arose and my clenched fist boldly thumped onto my chest. The unity between our brethren and blood presented itself as everyone followed my example, showing the utmost respect for the ideals that captivated our souls.

"I solemnly swear to you, my brothers and sisters, that I will forever place the fundamentals and exigencies of our people before my own." Reed's voice boomed with maturity and valor as he spoke before us. "I will protect our people, even if my life is laid to rest for that to be achieved. I will honor my father's legacy and create my own for centuries to come. I, Reed Lanthir, will uphold the responsibilities and duties of a monarch in the name of our ancestors."

Cheers exploded uproariously from the hearts of our elvish colony. Reed's words deeply connected with everyone who heard him. I felt my eyes burn with tears as a vivid memory of my childhood flashed before me. For a brief moment, Reed disappeared, and before me stood a young boy with a tender flush face and a radiant carefree smile spread ear to ear. Over the course of many years, I had watched my older brother transform before my eyes, like a tree stretching its branches towards the sun. From the mischievous boy who once led daring escapades, he blossomed into a steadfast man of wisdom and resilience. The rough edges of youth were smoothed away, revealing a deeper understanding of the world and a quiet strength that held our family together. As the seasons passed, I witnessed him navigate challenges with unwavering determination, his shoulders bearing the weight of responsibility without faltering. The sparkle of his eyes once filled with youthful mischief, now reflected the wisdom he had earned through experience. His laughter resonated like a comforting melody, a testament to the laughter and tears we had shared. In his growth, I saw a reflection of the bonds that tied us, the journey that had shaped us, and the promise of a future built on the foundation of our shared history. My eyes could no longer hold the weight of the rivers that were now flowing down my cheeks.

What a fine young man my brother had grown into, I thought, wiping away the tears on my cheeks.

Without another moment to think, Reed ran to me and wrapped his arms around me firmly, as if he knew what I was thinking. I smiled, warmed in the cocoon of my older brother's embrace, and let the world's worries melt away. His arms, a fortress of comfort, encircled me with a sense of security that transcended words. Every worry, every fear, seemed to dissipate against his strength, as if his hug could chase away even the darkest of shadows. In that moment, I felt cherished, understood, and safe—wrapped in a bond that had weathered the storms of time. His heartbeat echoed like a steady drum, a rhythm that reminded me of our shared journey and the unbreakable ties that bound us.

"Thank you, Ilana. Thank you for coming back to us," Reed said, eyes hazy with tears.

"I would never abandon my family," I replied, trying to keep my tears from staining his shirt.

"I'm grateful that this world hasn't carried you away. I was so scared before, that you wouldn't wake." Reed's words were shaky as he finally let down his armor to show the wounds he endured.

"I know, I am deeply sorry for any pain that I have caused-" I started before Reed cut me off.

"No," Reed said, cutting me off. "Thanks to you, our colony has found strength through the shadows of chaos. We would have been doomed to the evils of this world if not for what you have done." He sounded proud.

I felt both embarrassed and relieved as he spoke, surprised by his composure. At that moment, I knew my father was proud of us for who we had become. I wished he could be there, to tell us himself, to assuage the lingering doubt in my mind, but I could, at that moment at least, be certain. He was proud of us.

I smiled at the world around me, knowing that I was slowly finding myself. I vowed that I would continue to put the puzzle pieces of my identity together as I continued to grow, even in the grimmest moments that were predicted to occur in the future before us.

"Ilana, you too have grown into a prodigious elf. You have a power stronger than you know. You have hope and desire to chase what you believe in, despite the risks and the odds. Never give that up for anyone or anything, understand?"

Reed's face shone in the rays of the sun as if my father was speaking through him. I couldn't help but shed a tear at the thought of my father giving me advice one more time before he rested.

"I swear to you, I refuse to lose that attribute. You have my word." I spoke softly, but it was not only my brother I promised.

I turned to face our sacred tree and I smiled. I reached my arm out as I slowly stepped closer and gently put my hand on its rough, but remarkably gentle bark. Beneath the sprawling branches of the ancient tree that bore witness to the passage of countless ages, I felt a profound gratitude that seemed to emanate from the very essence of my being. Its gnarled roots, firmly anchored in the earth, whispered tales of elven history and ancestral souls, stories that resonated with the wisdom of ages past. In its rugged bark and outstretched limbs, I saw the embodiment of our lineage, a living testament to the journeys undertaken by those who came before. Each rustling leaf seemed to echo the laughter and tears of generations, a melody woven into the fabric of time. My heart swelled with reverence for this sentinel of memory, a guardian of the stories that shaped our people. In its shade, I found solace and a deep sense of connection, a reminder that I was but a single thread in the grand tapestry of elven existence. My thoughts of thankfulness radiated from my scintillating eyes as a familiar hand rested itself gently upon my shoulder. I glanced over to see Merlin smiling at me. The smile didn't last, dropping away to somber contemplation.

"Merlin, what's troubling you?" I asked, tenderly.

"During our fight against Alastor, I saw someone," Merlin's voice was almost shaky with dread. "I saw my brother, Talon. I don't know what to think or how to feel."

"Didn't he go missing, according to your father?" I asked, cautiously.

"That's... that's what we thought. I never could have imagined he would have gotten caught up with someone as cruel as Alastor," he said, his eyes narrowed with concern and ire.

As I looked into Merlin's eyes, I could feel the weight of his turmoil, the storm of emotions that raged within him. The confusion etched on his face mirrored the conflicted state of his heart, a heart torn between the bond of blood and the stark reality of betrayal. Sorrow radiated from him like a palpable aura, a tangible manifestation of the pain he must have felt witnessing his own brother standing on the side of darkness. At that moment, our connection stretched beyond words; I understood the ache that gnawed at his soul, the helplessness that carved at his resolve. My heart went out to him, for his suffering transcended the confines of right and wrong, reaching into the depths of a brotherly love overshadowed by a treacherous twist of fate.

"There has to be a good reason for his actions. It won't do us any good to assume outcomes that we don't have clues towards," I offered, hoping to settle his woes, at least for a moment.

"I understand what you're trying to say, Lala. However, even if his intentions are good, he tried to harm you and your people. I don't know if I can forgive that." As Merlin spoke, a profound ache tugged at my heart, urging me to offer solace in his time of need. Yet, the words I sought eluded me, slipping through my fingers like grains of sand. I yearned to help him, but words failed me. All I could do was stand there, silent, my heart aching in solidarity with him, unable to do anything but watch.

"Maybe there's more to it," I whispered, but even before Merlin shook his head, I knew it was fruitless.

"How could we find out?"

Even knowing it was coming, I didn't have an answer.

Merlin's gaze fell to his feet as he pondered endlessly about his brother. I felt deep sorrow for Merlin, but at the same time, I wondered if Talon was a contrite soul.

"We all have made mistakes," I tried. "Surely… we can't just jump to condemning him." I took his hands and urged him to look back up at me. "It's not over yet."

"I know," he whispered. Then, even quieter, "I'm scared."

He was searching for a safe haven and comfort as the tides of restless waters tried to pull him into an ocean of confusion. I offered him my tight embrace to pull him from the depths of his mind, and warm fountains spouted from his eyes. I felt his turmoil fall over me as if it were a blanket of thorns.

"We will find him, I promise you," I vowed boldly, holding his tender face in my delicate hands.

"How?" Merlin asked, a voice full of hopelessness.

"We will figure it out," I declared, "and we will do this together."

"You're both going to need these if you wish to find what you seek." My brother's sudden interjection startled me, causing me to jump.

He reached his hands out, and a chartreuse green magic encased them. A gust of wind circled around us, and two miniature rock golems burst from the ground. As they rose to their feet, their eyes, and a single rune-like swirl that branded their torso, began to glow the same hue as my brother's magic. I crouched down to meet its gaze and I stared at it in astonishment. I giggled while I gently patted one of them on the head causing it to make an affable noise, seeming to radiate an appreciative smile from its eyes since it didn't have a mouth.

"That one is Graggle," Reed started as he pointed at the golem closest to me, "and over there is Groggle. They are tracking golems. Hopefully, you will find them helpful."

"They are adorable! I didn't know that you had the ability to create beings like this," I exclaimed, awestruck by my brother's magic.

"I've been around a long time, I've picked up a few things here and there," he responded with a wink.

"Hey now, you're not *that* old!" I joked as I gently punched his shoulder.

"Wow, the resemblance between you and Vulcan is incredible," Merlin chuckled as he spoke to Reed.

"I highly doubt that," Reed denied.

"How will they help us find Talon?"

"They track magic, much like a scent hound would track a scent. All they need is an item of his," Reed said, informatively.

"Unfortunately, we don't have anything of the sort," Merlin said as his face fell once again.

"You don't, but I do." Reed's words struck Merlin and me like lightning, both surprising and confusing us.

"What do you mean?" I asked, confusedly.

Without another word, Reed snapped his fingers and a small bud sprouted elegantly from the earth. As it slowly opened, a meager piece of charcoal gray cloth, identical to Talon's hood, fluttered to our feet. Graggle slowly leaned over to carefully gather the cloth in its coarse palms. It turned the cloth slowly through its stubby fingers, before letting out a low bellow.

"All there is to do now is follow the golems."

"How did you know to hold onto the cloth?"

"Ilana, I know you and I know that staying here ruling this colony is a penitentiary for you," Reed started before gently cupping my hands in his. "This is your home, not your prison. You have the heart of a winged beast, longing for adventure and wonder."

I felt my face flush as my flustered expression caused both Merlin and Reed to chuckle. For the first time in my life, I felt as if the chains that once bound me to my duties had been vanquished.

"I love you, dear brother." I whimpered graciously as I wrapped my arms around him.

"I'm going to miss you," Reed started as tears once again plagued his vision. "Don't grow up too much while you're away, you're still my little sister after all."

"I'm going to miss you as well, and I promise I won't. We both know that I'm a child at heart."

"While you both are on your journey to find Talon, would you please investigate the growing darkness that looms overhead?" Reed asked, earnestly.

"Of course. We need to figure out what we are up against." I replied, gingerly.

"Reed," Merlin started as he turned to face my brother, "I'm truly grateful, thank you."

But Reed just shook his head lightly as he smiled, "Take good care of Ilana for me, will you?"

"Of course, you have my word," Merlin replied, honorably.

"Hey, I can also take care of myself, you know!" I joked light-heartedly.

All three of us laughed as we gently came together for a group embrace. I smiled to myself, knowing that the bad blood between humans and elves was finally fading away. We were one step closer to peace.

As we pulled away from one another, my brother turned to face the crowd of elves who were now conversing amongst themselves and announced, "People of Aefaradiron, it is with both pride and a heavy heart that I announce the departure of my dear sister, Princess Ilana Lanthir, and Prince Merlin Grimald."

Gasps could be heard rising from the crowd that stood before us, followed by the echoes of murmurs. A diminutive wave of nervousness fell over me once again, but I quickly shook it away as I locked arms with Merlin.

"Do not fret, they will return in due time. There is a growing threat beyond our boundaries." Reed's voice went from light-hearted to serious within moments, "These two have bravely and generously volunteered to investigate the growing infection of violence that has begun to scourge our world."

"My people, I pledge an oath of purity as I journey through unfamiliar territories. I will bring peace to this land once again," I said, confidently as determination filled every fiber of my being.

An uproar of cheers, like a massive tidal wave of exultation, flooded our colony. Laughter and applause intermingled, a symphony of celebration that infused the atmosphere with a contagious energy. Amid the uproar, it was as if time momentarily stood still, allowing everyone to bask in the sheer delight of the moment. I smiled and brought my right hand to my chest and lifted my left hand to the sky. The sun's radiant rays illuminated the earth around us as if the world itself approved of our ideals.

"Be safe you two," Reed urged, hours later, as we stood at the edge of the colony. Everyone had come to see us off, but they had slowly trickled away until only Reed remained.

"We will, I promise. Take care of our people." I patted his arm. "And take care of yourself."

He huffed a small laugh, then pulled me into one last hug. He ruffled my hair, then turned back to the colony. For a moment, I watched him go.

As my final words to my brother sank in, I felt both sadness and determination fill my mind. As I prepared to embark on my journey, my heart weighed heavy with the knowledge that my departure meant leaving my beloved brother behind to face the duties of kinghood on his own. The bond we shared, woven through years of shared laughter, whispered secrets, and unspoken understandings, felt like an intricate tapestry that I was reluctantly unraveling. The thought of his absence, of the daily rituals and familiar presence I would no longer have once again, tugged at my emotions like a gentle ache. Each memory we had created together seemed to echo in the corners of my mind, a testament to the depth of our connection. The prospect of navigating uncharted territories without his steady companionship was both exhilarating and bittersweet, a reminder that even in my pursuit of new horizons, the comfort of my older brother's presence would be deeply missed. Though, this was not goodbye, it was I'll see you later after our quest is complete. I worried for my brother, however I knew he was as tough as nails and braver than the lions that prowled the earth. I felt the stares of my people burn into my back as we began towards the forest where our paths first intertwined.

Then I turned to face Merlin. "So," I said, taking his hand, "where should we start?"

"We must return to where it all began, where he disappeared. Camelot."

So it would be the same trip once again. I adjusted the pack I had slung over my shoulder.

Deja vu pierced my mind as a younger and more innocent version of myself stared at me with an adventurous grin. Embarking on this voyage that bore a striking resemblance to the beginning of a once-new chapter in life instantly stirred a rush of memories. The familiarity of the setting, the scent in the air, or even a fleeting sensation seemed to summon the echoes of the past. It was as if time folded upon itself, intertwining the threads of the present with the tapestry of the past. Each sight and sound became a trigger, pulling fragments of recollections to the forefront of my mind, a vivid reminder of the experiences that had paved the way for my current adventure. In these moments, the past and present seemed to converge, creating a bridge between the years and evoking emotions that had once marked the start of a new era. It was fascinating how a few weeks can seem like an eternity. Having journeyed a considerable distance in what felt like the blink of an eye, I found myself standing at a crossroads of emotions. A sense of accomplishment swelled within me, mingling with a tinge of astonishment at how swiftly the path had unfolded. Yet, as I looked ahead, a mixture of eagerness and nervous anticipation bloomed within my heart. The road that stretched before me was shrouded in mystery, its twists and turns veiled in the haze of the unknown. The steady progression of time seemed to propel me forward, like a current carrying me toward uncharted territories. With each step, I carried the lessons of the past and the hopes of the future, a constant reminder that the journey itself was a destination worth cherishing. As I stood on the precipice of what lay ahead, I couldn't help but wonder how much farther I would go, how much more I would learn, and how many more milestones I would reach as time continued its relentless march.

"Are you ready?" Merlin asked, looking at me.

"As long as I'm with you, I'm ready for anything," I replied assuredly with conviction.

With a smile on our faces, we began our journey once again, similar to the path in which we started. *Tempora mutantur et nos mutamur in illis.*

"The times are changing, and we change in them."